Sunset Serenade

ANJ
Press

Pittsburgh

SUNSET SERENADE

ANJ Press, First edition. NOV 2023.

Copyright © 2023 Amelia Addler.

Written by Amelia Addler.

Cover design by CrocoDesigns

Maps by MistyBeee

For facing our fears

Recap and Introduction to
Sunset Serenade

Welcome back to Orcas Island! Last year, Claire Cooke bought The Grand Madrona Hotel and fell in love with both the island and the hotel manager, Chip Douglas.

Claire's luck didn't stop there. Her daughters followed her to the island, one by one. First was Lucy with her fiery personality, going after any wrong-doers and finally meeting her match in Rob. Lillian was next, thrilled to reconnect with her high school sweetheart, Dustin.

Lillian's twin Rose is the last to succumb to the island's charm. She's running away from San Francisco after getting fired from a – let's face it – terrible job. She's hoping to find her confidence again, but she might get more than she bargained for after a case of mistaken identity gets her a job offer she can't refuse – as a matchmaker!

The only match she's not able to predict is her own as she finds herself falling in love with her boss...

STUART
ISLAND

WALDRON
ISLAND

ORCAS
ISLAND

SPIEDEN
ISLAND

POSEY
ISLAND

CYPRESS
ISLAND

SHAW
ISLAND

SAN JUAN
ISLAND

BLAKELY
ISLAND

DECATUR
ISLAND

LOPEZ
ISLAND

ANACORTES

N
W · E
S

THE SAN JUAN ISLANDS

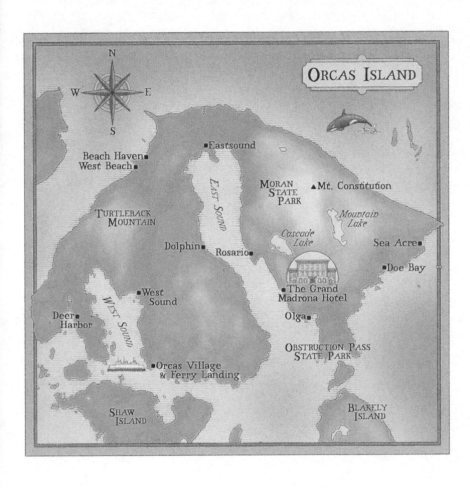

Chapter One

I n the middle of a newsroom, under lights more intense than the midday sun, it dawned on Rose that her self-doubt was an infection she'd ignored for far too long, and suddenly, she was going septic.

She watched as someone clipped a microphone onto the lapel of her suit jacket – so small and light, like a butterfly resting its wings.

Importantly, however, it was not a butterfly, and its wings would soon broadcast her voice to the good people of the Seattle metro area – all 3.5 million of them.

She gaped down at it, and a man wearing a headset stopped what he was doing to point at her. "No mouth breathing. Your mic is live."

Her head shot up and she clamped her jaw shut. "Sorry!"

He yelled out, "In five, four, three..."

His voice trailed off, finishing counting with his fingers struck into the air.

Rose smiled blankly ahead, a deer in the headlights – or in this case, a deer about to be interviewed on the news about a book titled *Find Your Perfect Match: Data and insights from decades of relationship research.*

Not only had she not written the book, she had never read the book, or even *heard* of it.

How had she ended up here?

The day had started off so well. Rose got up at five, determined to get to her job interview early, to get ready without waking her sisters.

Yet, when she got out of the shower, Lucy was in the kitchen frying bacon and eggs, a pot of fresh coffee at her side.

"You're really not going to take the ferry? It usually comes." Lucy paused. "Eventually."

"I can't risk it," Rose said.

As pleasant as ferry rides were, the chance of getting delayed was *way* too high. Rose despised being late. It made her sweaty and nervous and entirely not interview-ready.

There was no room for her to fail. Rose needed a job, a *real* job, not like the one Lucy had gotten her at the farm.

She was broke. As fun as living with her sisters and riding on the ferry was, she needed to get back to reality, and that meant moving back to the mainland where the jobs were. It was not the time to be whimsical and wish ferries ran on time or that she could live on Orcas Island forever.

She kept telling herself this, trying to make herself believe it.

"Your interview isn't until one," Lucy argued, popping the lid onto a travel mug and handing it to Rose. "I'm sure a ferry will show up before then."

Lillian shuffled into the kitchen and took a seat at the table, pulling her robe tightly across her chest. "Rose is turning into an old lady with her need to be early. I'm surprised she didn't book a hotel room so she could wake up in Seattle."

Rose had thought of doing that, but she couldn't afford a hotel room and was too proud to ask for money. "Don't be ridiculous," she scoffed. "I just need to make a good first impression."

"Why are you so anxious?" Lucy set down a basket over-flowing with warm slices of buttered brioche. "They'd be lucky to have you work for them."

"Yeah, right." Rose stared at the bread. She didn't want to have any. She didn't *need* to have any. She was cutting back on carbs. Ever since moving to the island, she'd felt the urge to reinvent herself, to live as she'd always wanted to live – and she'd feel ready to do that once she lost the extra pounds that had snuck on over the last few years.

What was one day, though?

She reached forward and grabbed a slice, bringing it close to her nose to breathe in the smell.

"Seriously." Lillian put a hand on Rose's shoulder. "You need to believe in yourself."

Easier said than done. Especially with the recent firing she'd endured from her last job. "I'll get right on that."

"I know you don't have much faith in yourself," Lucy said, loading Rose's plate with eggs and bacon. "You'll have to borrow mine. You're awesome! You're a super hard worker – you work *too* hard, actually – and people love you. What more could they want?"

Lillian nodded. "I agree with Lucy. You're a catch, and if they can't see that, you don't want to work for them anyway."

Rose couldn't stomach any more of their peppiness. She shoved a few forkfuls of egg into her mouth and stood. "I'll make sure to tell them that at the end of the interview."

"Lucy would," Lillian said with a laugh. "She'd give them a stern lecture on why they would be fools not to hire her."

Lucy nodded. "Confidence is the way, young grasshopper."

"I'm not sure that would work for me," Rose said.

"Right, that kind of attitude doesn't work for people-pleasers," Lucy added, then paused. "Sorry, but it's true."

Rose wished she was more like her sister: Bold. Poised. Fulfilled.

She didn't even need to be *all* of those things. She'd settle for a chance at being happy.

It didn't matter how hard she wished, though. "Ha, yeah. I know."

She pulled on her suit jacket and buttoned the center button, then quickly unbuttoned it when it restricted her breathing.

She didn't remember it being so tight. Had it shrunk? There was that picture from last weekend where she looked... *bigger.* Maybe those extra few pounds had really been an extra ten pounds. Or an extra twenty...

Ugh. Rose had a complicated relationship with food, she knew that. She was trying to get better.

Still, she hated pictures. They could ruin her day, or an entire weekend. She could be feeling *really* good about herself, and then a picture would appear and she started to question everything.

There wasn't time to get worked up about any of it now. She let out a sigh. "I'd better go. Thanks for breakfast."

"Good luck!" Lillian called out.

She slipped out of their apartment and into the cool morning air. It was crisp, and she felt a pang of sadness as she reached her dew-kissed car.

A job on the mainland meant leaving this beautiful island behind, with its twisted, red-barked trees, its miles of rocky beaches, and its far-reaching view of the sea from the mountaintop that was only a short drive from her apartment. It meant moving away from her mom and her sisters. It meant starting over.

Maybe that was what she needed? A new beginning. To go out on her own, find her own strength. To get away from Lucy's lavish breakfasts, at the very least, for the sake of her increasingly tight professional wardrobe.

Eighties music blasted through the radio as Rose drove on, under the branches of the looming trees in Moran State Park, through the sleepy town of Eastsound, and on to the little airport where the small prop plane awaited its passengers.

Rose was one of four flying out that morning, and the pilot was inside the airport. It was a casual scene, with him leaning against the counter and eating a donut, laughing about a recent incident where the sheriff's deputies were dispatched to catch a loose pair of baby goats.

"The goats led them to a stolen golf cart," the pilot said. "I think they should be made into honorary deputies."

Rose smiled to herself. The small-town squabbles were her favorite. She'd spent the last eight years in San Francisco, and while she thought she'd miss the bustle of the city, it had yet to hit her.

At least, if she worked in Seattle, she could still visit on the weekends. That's what she told herself as they boarded the plane, the sun cracking the horizon. She repeated it as they took off, the islands scattered beneath them, dotted with green trees and kissed by the golden morning light.

They landed in Seattle early, leaving Rose five hours to kill before her interview. She wandered to Pike Place Market, determined to resist buying any snacks and wishing she'd brought her camera so she could take pictures.

There were rows upon rows of flowers in every color, yellow and red and blue and white. Some of the stalls were open, some not, and the tourists hadn't yet filled the space with their excitement.

Rose managed to make it an hour and a half before wandering into a French bakery and buying a bag of chouquettes, the delicate little puffs of dough so delightfully covered in sugar. She decided to bring half home to share, and half could be her treat for interview day.

By eleven, she was anxious to get to the building where the interview would take place. Sure, she'd be two hours early, but she could check in, get past security, and read a book somewhere.

It took thirty minutes to get there, and stepping into the lobby of the high rise gave her a jolt of excitement. People walked quickly, talking to one another, on their phones, or with their arms stacked with coffee or boxes.

Rose walked up to the security desk and waited in line for thirteen minutes – again grateful she'd come early – before getting to the front and presenting her ID to the security guard.

The man's eyes popped a little when he saw her name. "I got a call they were waiting for you," he said, standing from his seat. "Come with me. I'll take you up."

How had she kept them waiting? She was still an hour early.

Rose felt so embarrassed that she didn't question it. She rushed up to the twelfth floor, though she was pretty certain she was supposed to be on the third. When a woman asked her if she was here for the interview, she said yes and didn't question why she was hurried into a makeup chair, her face dabbed with this and that.

Rose wasn't one to question things. She assumed other people knew better than she did, that she must have missed something, and surely there was a reason they were sitting her in front of a camera.

It had to be part of the interview. A test. There had to be a reason, and it only evaded her because she had missed a detail, some crucial email, perhaps.

Clearly, there was no self-doubt too far-fetched for Rose to believe.

The screen in front of her lit up with a dazzlingly beautiful news anchor. "We are so happy to have you on the show today, Rose. I'm sorry, Dr. Woodson. Do you mind if I call you Rose?"

Her heart dropped into her stomach. Something had gone wrong. *Very* wrong. She was not supposed to be here. She didn't know what this was, but it was not an interview for an administrative assistant job. She was not a doctor, her last name was Wood*ley*, and her suit jacket might actually be trying to strangle her to death.

Yet it was happening, and it couldn't have happened to a more perfect victim. She was panicking, and when Rose panicked, her mind went blank. It was like the white light people talk about when they have a near-death experience: bright, blinding, and all-encompassing.

Rose blinked rapidly and forced a smile. "Of course! Call me Rose. Just Rose. Thank you for having me."

Chapter Two

"You all right?"

Craig's eyes shot up from his half-eaten sub. "Me? Yeah. I'm good, thanks."

"If they messed it up..." The waitress motioned to his plate. "We'll make you another one. You don't have to torture yourself."

Craig laughed. He'd forgotten he was in public. He knew better than to hunch his shoulders down like this, sighing and grimacing. "The sandwich isn't torture. It's great." He nodded his head down to his phone. "Work is...the problem."

She eyed him for a moment, then smiled. "All right. Good. More coffee?"

"Please."

She topped off his mug and disappeared.

Work. Work was always the problem.

Craig took a swig, savoring the slightly caramel tones. He loved this diner. It was right next to the office, and their coffee was always fresh and cheap.

The food was always good, too. Consistent. Whenever it started to feel like the pressure was building up at work, like he was going to combust with one more request, Craig escaped and sat at this counter. Coffee. A sandwich. A slice of pie, sometimes, if he had the stomach for it.

Today he didn't. He'd spent the morning in meetings, acting like everything was fine.

It wasn't. How many years now had it been? How many years had he felt like a college kid pretending to be a COO? Through the rounds of funding, the years of expansion. Their dating app had gone from a few users to a few hundred to a few *million*.

It didn't matter how he felt. He *was* COO. People counted on him. His company provided their livelihoods. These people actually knew what they were doing – analysts, coders, accountants. They didn't deserve to lose everything because he couldn't keep faking competence.

Craig sighed. Something had to change. He didn't know what, or how, but he had to figure it out.

It was precisely at that moment that he sat back and something—rather, someone—on the TV caught his eye.

Was it her bright smile? Her calm, intelligent demeanor? Or the description under her name: *Relationship Expert.*

Why hadn't he thought of finding a relationship expert?

"Hey," Craig called out, "can you turn that up?"

The waitress nodded and increased the volume.

It was a local news program – not something Craig normally watched. He didn't have time to watch TV anymore.

The newscaster sat at a desk, her hands clasped in an eager sort of way. "What got you interested in the science of relationships?"

"Well..." The woman paused, nodding slowly, her shining dark hair reflecting light. "I've always been a romantic. A believer in true love, if you will."

"That doesn't sound very scientific," the interviewer said with a laugh.

The woman smiled and paused again. "No. Like my twin sister always says, your choice of a romantic partner is the most important decision you'll ever make. It needs to be based in reason."

A researcher who took romantic whimsy and paired it with theory?

Craig leaned in, narrowing his eyes.

"Your twin?" The interviewer touched a hand to her chest. "Now there's an important relationship."

Craig looked at the name at the bottom of the screen – Dr. Rose Woodson, PhD, MFCC, author of *Find Your Perfect Match*.

"Absolutely. She knows me better than I know myself, sometimes."

This was it. The answer he'd been looking for, the *person* he didn't know he needed.

Craig snapped a picture of his screen and sent it to his assistant Lydia.

"Who's this?" she texted back a moment later.

It was too much to type, so he called her. "Hey, it's me."

"I know. What's up boss?"

"There's a psychologist on KPXI 11 right now. Rose some-thing...Rose Woodman? Can you grab her and tell her I need to talk to her?"

Their office was in the same building as KPXI, so it wouldn't be too hard to catch her. Or, at least, he hoped it wouldn't be.

"Sure, leaving now. What do you want me to say to her?"

Craig threw a fifty onto the counter and stood, grabbing his coat. "Tell her she's got a job at SerenadeMe and I won't take no for an answer."

Chapter Three

After four minutes of rambling, the questions stopped, the microphone disappeared, and Rose was escorted back to the elevator.

"Thanks for your time today." The woman flashed a smile as she pushed the "L" button.

Without a word, Rose got on, then stood staring, like cattle going to slaughter.

Of course, the slaughter had already happened.

The doors started closing on her face as she called out, "You too!"

The doors shut, and embarrassment washed over her. "You too?" she muttered to herself, shaking her head.

What had she even said during that interview? It was like she'd entered a fugue state and her subconscious had taken over. She had the vague memory of being fueled by Lillian and Lucy's delusional praise but couldn't remember a single full sentence that had come out of her mouth.

She could've told them anything. She may have rattled off her social security number, or where her ex-boyfriend had taken her on their last date, or a confession about a cupcake she'd stolen when she was seven.

The elevator dinged, the doors opening to the lobby.

Rose ran her hands over her suit jacket and took a breath. Whatever she'd said, it didn't matter. It wasn't her job interview – *that* she was sure of – so it wasn't her problem. It was their problem once they figured out they'd gotten the wrong person.

Yeah. She had other things to worry about.

The doors opened and she walked out, catching sight of herself in the shining doors of the elevator across the hall. They were like a mirror, reflecting back her businesswoman look and the fake glasses she'd worn to look smart.

It had worked, apparently. Too well. They thought she had written a book. On love!

Rose let out a laugh, covering her mouth. It was too absurd to make up. Lillian and Lucy wouldn't even believe her when she told them later.

She kept walking, weaving through the building's lower lobby, a six-foot tall digital clock towering over her and counting away the time – 12:53.

Her stomach sank. She was about to be late for her other interview, the one she'd meant to do, the one she was qualified for – or at least, she *hoped* she was qualified for – and it was entirely her fault for not speaking up and simply saying, "Oh no, I was not supposed to be interviewed on the news about writing a book, but thank you."

At least it was over. She still had a chance to make it on time, and her hair looked *really* good.

She darted back into the waiting elevator and pressed the button for the third floor.

Nothing.

She pressed it again, and a screen flashed "scan badge."

"Shoot." She stepped out, looking for the friendly security guard who had rushed her upstairs before. She spotted him at his desk, with a line of people waiting in front of him.

She had no choice but to go and get to the back of the line.

Rose arrived for her interview sweaty and short of breath, six minutes after it was supposed to begin.

Her potential boss, an unsmiling man in his fifties, led her into a conference room and sat down with a huff. "This is not a good start for someone who boasted about their organization skills in their cover letter."

"I know, and I am *so* sorry. You wouldn't believe what happened."

He held up a hand. "I don't care. Let's get this over with."

~

Seventeen minutes later, she was back in the lobby, looking down at her feet and trudging through the crowd. She had a sinking feeling in her gut, telling her everything that had happened was her fault. The last thing she wanted to do was deal with that feeling.

She needed a distraction. Rose pulled out her phone and saw a text from Lillian.

How'd it go??

Not the kind of distraction she was looking for. She put her phone away, her eye catching a Starbucks across the lobby.

Perfect.

The line was long, but that was okay with Rose. It would give her time to carefully consider what she was going to order. A pumpkin spice latte was always nice, but there was a new apple cider tea concoction she'd wanted to try, and who knew when she'd be near a Starbucks again. There were none on Orcas Island, and it didn't seem like she'd be starting a new job any time soon.

A soft voice chimed behind her. "Dr. Woodson?"

Rose paused her careful drink consideration and stood still, listening.

Was the real Dr. Woodson nearby? Was she about to get yelled at for stealing her identity?

"Rose?"

She peered over her shoulder and spotted a woman looking at her. She was young and slight, wearing a black dress with a shining gold belt, and she smiled brightly when Rose looked at her.

Rose forced a smile back. "Hi."

The young woman took a step toward her. "I'm so glad I found you. My name is Lydia, and my boss wanted me to catch you before you left. He wants to talk to you."

The line was moving. Rose was third, and she still hadn't made up her mind on what she wanted to order. "Sorry. I'm in a hurry."

"He wanted me to tell you he has a job for you."

Rose stopped. "A job?"

"Yes! He's on his way. Should be here *any* minute." She frowned and added, "Please don't leave."

"You're his... assistant?"

She nodded, the desperation plain on her face.

Rose knew the feeling, and the job, well. Her last position as an administrative assistant had gone from wonderful to torturous. She wasn't sure when the change had happened, but looking back made it obvious that things had been bad for a while.

"Okay. I won't leave." Rose sighed. "I'm going to get a pumpkin spice latte. Do you want one?"

Lydia shook her head. "No, but thank you."

Rose never used to accept treats at work, either. It felt like the right thing to do – to deny that she would like a donut, or a coffee, or enough time between meetings to run to the bathroom.

What had she been trying to prove? Her dedication? Her worth? That she was a machine who would do anything for the company, no matter how tired she was, and despite the fact she'd worked seven weekends in a row without a single day off?

A fat lot of good that did. They'd fired her anyway. After eight years of toil and devotion, one random Tuesday morning she looked up from her desk to see security standing over her, telling her to pack her things.

She got to the front of the line and placed her order, then stepped aside, the memories churning within her. It had been months since she'd gotten fired, yet the nausea hit as if she was staring into that little box of her belongings again, blinking back tears as she walked past her coworkers, unable to make eye contact with anyone.

"Two pumpkin spice lattes for Rose!" the barista called out.

"Thank you," she said with a smile, accepting them before walking back to Lydia. "I got you one anyway, and I'm sorry if you wanted something else, but you really should've told me."

Lydia laughed, accepting the green-and-white cup. "Wow, thank you. I love pumpkin spice lattes."

"I know, right? Everyone makes fun of it but they're *so* good. What're you supposed to do? *Not* enjoy them?"

"Right. They taste better than being smug feels." She smiled, taking a sip before sticking her hand into the air and waving. "Oh, he's here!"

Rose turned and spotted a suit-clad man walking toward them. He had short black hair and a neatly trimmed beard, and his dark grey suit jacket hung open in a casual sort of way. His expression was hard, his mouth set in a line, and his eyes focused on Rose.

He didn't look like the type who took *no* for an answer.

"Do you like working for him?" Rose said under her breath.

"Yes, I do."

She leaned closer, dropping her voice to a whisper. "I mean *really*. Is your life falling apart because of your job being too demanding and him asking too much?"

Her eyes widened. "Not at all. I love this job, and the company. It's awesome!"

An unconvincing answer. Rose might've said the same thing a few years ago, before she had been hit by a tidal wave of humiliation from an unceremonious sacking.

He reached them and extended a handshake. "Hi. I'm Craig Mitchell."

Rose accepted it with a nod. "Nice to meet you."

"I just saw your interview on KPXI and I was blown away."

"Ha." Rose clenched her coffee with both hands. "Thanks."

"I'm not going to waste your time. I'd like to offer you a job at my company."

She raised an eyebrow. "Uh, that's nice, but – "

He put his hands up. "Before you say no, give me a chance to tell you more about what you'd be doing."

She stared at him, his hazel eyes wide and full of hope. As badly as she needed a job, she couldn't keep pretending to be Rose Woodson, PhD, when she was just Rose Woodley with a bachelors in biology and a too-tight jacket.

Rose shook her head. "I'm sorry, but I really need to be going."

"You don't have to answer yet. Let me walk with you. I'm going to make you an offer you can't refuse."

He smiled, the edges reaching his eyes and wrinkling at the corners.

Did he know how bad she was at saying no? Because it seemed like he knew exactly how hard this was for her.

Rose shook her head and opened her mouth, but nothing came out.

He spoke again. "What do you have to lose?"

Craig and Lydia stared at her, the heat of their attention burning her skin. She knew what they wanted her to say. She knew what the easy answer was, what would get them to stop looking at her, and she knew what she was supposed to say: a clear, resounding *no*.

She took a sip of her latte. The whipped cream had melted away. "Okay," she finally said.

He clapped his hands together. "Okay!"

The tension in her chest dissipated, and she chanced another sip of her drink. She quite liked the melted whipped cream, and at least they weren't looking at her anymore. She would get out of this debacle sooner or later.

Yeah. Soon enough, she'd get away from this disaster of a day, and it'd all be a funny story to tell back on the island.

Chapter Four

There was no point in trying to lowball her. The company needed her, and no one else would do. Craig was sure of it. He could feel it in his chest.

"Let me start with what we can offer," Craig said as they walked through the lobby. "Your salary would start at two hundred thousand a year, in addition to stock and profit-sharing distributions."

"Two hundred thousand?" Rose repeated, her eyes fixed on the coffee in her hands.

"I know. With rent prices in Seattle, it's not the most competitive. But that doesn't include bonuses, which are given out quarterly."

She nodded, walking through the lobby doors and onto the sidewalk. Her pace was slow and methodical, like she was considering what he had to say.

Or so he hoped. "We have a gym on site, a meditation studio, daily catered lunches, and a fully-funded pension. The health insurance is top-of-the-line and provided at no cost to you."

Craig glanced at her, searching her face for any signs of interest.

There didn't seem to be any. The muscles in her face were tense and her eyes kept darting between the people they passed, the buildings, and the pavement beneath them. She looked pained, like she wanted to get away from him.

As much as he wanted to keep piling on the perks, it clearly wasn't working. He wasn't good at this. His business partner, Barney, would know what to do; he'd know how to woo her, he'd find the right things to say.

He wasn't around, though.

Craig could hear Barney's voice whispering in his mind: figure out what *she* wants and give that to her.

He stopped walking. "I'm sorry, I haven't given you a chance to talk."

"No, it's okay. I'm happy to listen." She looked at him for the first time since he'd started blathering, then quickly turned her eyes up, quiet and pensive. "I guess there's one question I have."

"Anything."

"What exactly does your company do?"

A laugh bellowed out of him and he put a hand over his mouth. "I'm so sorry. I thought my assistant already filled you in. I'm the COO for a company called SerenadeMe."

She bit her lip. "I don't know much about SerenadeMe."

"Right. I sometimes forget everyone doesn't live and breathe this stuff." He cleared his throat. This might be a harder sell than he'd anticipated, especially since he was so bad at selling. His mind buzzed, frantic, trying to come up with the right words. "SerenadeMe is a revolution for dating."

She cracked a smile. "A revolution?"

Craig couldn't help but laugh at himself again. "Sorry, sometimes I spend too much time with the PR department and start talking like one of them. I don't mean to. Let me start over.

"I'm not a business guy. I'm a coder. In college, me and my roommate Barnabas – Barney – started a project. Something for fun. We used a set of questions from a psychology paper about long-lasting relationships to pair up some of our class-mates for blind dates. We played matchmaker, just for fun, and people loved it. Before long, it spread across the campus, and long story short, we made it into a dating app called Sere-nadeMe."

"Ah. A dating app."

"Yes, with a twist. Our clients don't browse profiles. Our system takes their responses and finds them a match."

"A matchmaker dating app?" Rose looked down. "I think I have heard of this."

Now they were getting somewhere. "It's not as hokey as it sounds, I swear."

She laughed. "It doesn't sound hokey."

"I know it doesn't compare to what you do – research and actual scholarship – but with the app, we try to keep it based in reality. We get input from psychologists and relationship thera-pists. The matching technology – we've fine-tuned it, I guess. I mean, I don't guess, we have." Not going well. *Focus.* "For the most part, it works, but when I saw you on the news now – I mean, you just *get* it. You get it in a way none of our consultants ever have."

Rose took a deep breath. "Okay, listen, you should know that—"

"Wait! Before you say no. The reason we need you is because the company went public two years ago, and now the board wants to sell. We have a potential buyer, but he's not convinced we have anything special. Anything elite to justify the high price tag we're asking."

Anything to justify their high stock price, anything to prevent it from plummeting like the article in *The Times* said it would...

The lid to her coffee popped off, launching into the air and onto the sidewalk. "Oh my! I always have a death grip on my coffee," she said. "Sorry."

They both crouched down, almost bumping heads, with Rose pulling away at the last second. "I'm going to disappoint you, I'm afraid." She put the lid back on and straightened. "As much as I'd love to help, I can't do anything elite. The truth is..." Her voice trailed off, and she scratched her head. "When I went on that interview today–"

"I can get you a company car. Flights – we'll pay for flights. Whatever you want."

"I actually need to catch a flight right now," she said, looking at her wrist. "Oh. Forgot I don't have my watch today. Ha."

"You don't live in the city?" He straightened his shoulders. "We have free apartments for our employees downtown.

They're nothing fancy, but it's a nice place to relax if you need to come in for a meeting."

"I live on Orcas Island, actually. That's why this can't happen. Otherwise, I would *totally* love to work for you. Okay, thanks, got to run!"

She started walking again and Craig went after her. "I'm on Orcas all the time! I'm renovating a house for my parents' retirement. It's a great place – easy to travel here, actually. We'll cover all the flights you need. You can work from home most of the time, if you prefer. Problem solved."

She looked at him, scrunching her nose and pressing her lips together.

This was it. His last chance. It felt like the company was days away from falling apart, days left before the investors and employees and the board realized he was a fraud. That he'd been faking it this entire time.

Maybe it wasn't that close, but it felt that close, and the results would be disastrous.

And here! The solution had just walked into his life. He *knew* Rose was the answer. She felt so familiar, so genuine. Like she'd been part of his life – and his business – all this time.

He sighed and straightened his shoulders. "It won't be the sort of work you're used to; I know that. But you might still find it interesting. You'll pilot a new program for our clients. Our elite clients – you'll be their personal matchmaker. It's not like you'll go in blind – we have a ton of data. Tons of questions. It'll all be at your fingertips." He pulled out his card and handed it to her. "Here. I'm not going to pressure you. I'm a terrible salesman, and I apologize for that, but – I had to try, because you're remarkable, and I think you'd take us to the next level."

She laughed. "Yeah, thank you. Sorry, I just have to go."

"Think it over and give me a call. That's all I ask."

She accepted his card and stared at it in her hand for a beat. "Okay. I'll think about it."

"Thanks, Dr. Woodson."

"Please." She shook her head. "Call me Rose."

Craig grinned. Down to earth, too. "Rose. I look forward to hearing from you."

Chapter Five

"Let me get this straight," Lucy said, her arms crossed and her eyes narrowed. "This guy offered you a huge paycheck, a place to live, health insurance, free food, free flights – and you *didn't* say yes?"

Lillian hid her smile. Her sisters couldn't be more different and watching them trying to understand one another was a never-ending source of amusement.

"Are you even listening?" Rose let out a huff, her cheeks flushed. "He thought I was some famous psychologist. I can't keep pretending to be her."

"You never pretended to be her. He *assumed* it."

Rose shook her head. "Same thing."

"No, it's not," Lucy said. "Who's to say she's famous? She just wrote a book, and it's not like he read it."

Rose sighed and turned her gaze to Lillian. "Why aren't you saying anything?"

Uh oh. Her silence hadn't gone unnoticed.

Lillian put her hands up. "I'm trying to reserve judgement until we have all the facts."

Lucy groaned. "Come on. Don't act like this isn't the best thing that's ever fallen into Rose's lap." She paused. "Not to say you don't deserve it, Rose. What I mean is – it's long over-due for something good to happen to you."

Rose opened her mouth, shut it, and then frowned. "You think I'm pathetic, don't you?"

"No!" Lucy and Lillian said simultaneously.

Lucy softened her tone. "You deserve better than you've gotten, that's all."

Lillian nodded. "You've had a stretch of bad luck."

For the briefest of moments, it looked like Rose might have tears in her eyes, and Lillian could feel her throat tightening.

Her sister deserved far better treatment than she'd gotten at her last job. Lillian had believed that for years but could never convince Rose to leave. Rose always put the company first and put herself down. Her coworkers and boss hadn't helped – always happy to pile on the work and blame – and it became an unhealthy cycle.

It didn't help that no matter what Lillian did or said, she couldn't get Rose to believe in herself.

The moment passed and Rose looked up, rolling her eyes. "It's not bad luck when you do it to yourself. I could've quit way before they fired me."

"You weren't ready, and that's fine," Lucy said simply. "That wasn't your path. *This* is your path."

Lillian breathed in. Her sister's tears had passed, and so had hers. "Lucy's right. Maybe you were meant for this."

Rose's mouth popped open. "I can't believe you're agree-ing with her."

"Actually." Lucy turned, wide-eyed. "I can't either."

Lillian wasn't going to be the downer. Not this time.

She wanted to believe good things could happen, and she wanted them to happen for Rose. "Why shouldn't you take this job? He didn't say he wanted you for your expertise. He said he liked what you said in the interview, and to be fair, that was all you."

"If only I could remember what I said." Rose shook her head. "I've totally blocked it out."

"It must've come from the depths of your soul. I tried looking for it online, but they didn't have a clip up yet." Lucy waved a hand. "Whatever. It doesn't matter. You're into all that romance crap. You'll be a great matchmaker."

Rose sighed. "There's no way. I would be a fraud."

"It's not even a real job!" Lucy stood and started to pace the room. "He admitted he's trying to get someone impressive-looking so he can sell his business. All you have to do is play the part. You fooled him; you can fool whoever is buying the company, too."

"No. I can't." Rose pulled out her phone. "I'm going to text him and turn it down."

"Don't!" Lucy bellowed. "Take the win for once. Don't you think it'll be fun?"

She shrugged. "I mean, yeah. It sounds like the most fun job I've ever heard of."

"Might it make you happy?" Lucy asked.

A smile crossed Rose's face, and she let out a little laugh. "I don't know. I didn't even want to consider it – but yes, it might."

"Even Lillian," Lucy continued, pointing, "who *never* does anything fun or crazy, thinks you should do it."

It wasn't the time to argue she didn't do anything fun, but Lillian still shot Lucy a glare. "I mean, it *is* crazy. But it's sort of his fault for offering this job to a stranger."

"Exactly!" Lucy nodded excitedly.

"Plus, it's clear this company has a lot of money to throw around..." Lillian trailed off, aware that both Rose and Lucy were watching her.

Thinking of it, Lillian didn't care about the company or if they had money to spare. She cared about Rose, her overly-sweet people-pleasing sister who had gotten pushed down one too many times.

"I don't think you're hurting anyone by taking the job," Lillian finally said. "Craig told you himself – your position is something to seal a deal to sell the company. He's on his way out. What does he care? And it sounds so fun. It's an opportunity, one that seems perfect for you."

Rose's eyes brightened. "Do you really think so?"

Lillian smiled. "I do."

"I don't know." Rose shook her head. "What if the real Rose Woodson finds out? What if she sues me?"

"Sues you for what?" Lucy asked.

Lillian cut in. "She won't find out."

"She'll sue me for impersonating her and..." Rose shrugged. "Being happy."

That was it. Rose deserved to be happy, and she desperately wanted to accept the job. She just needed their permission for whatever reason.

"Why shouldn't you get to be happy?" Lillian clapped her hands together and pointed. "Pull out your phone. Right now. Call Craig and tell him you'll do it."

"Yes!" Lucy followed suit, clapping her hands. "Do it!"

"No, I can't!" Rose grinned from ear to ear, looking up at them coyly.

"Do it!" Lillian said.

She pulled out her phone and bit her lip. "Seriously? You guys think I can pull this off?"

"Rose," Lillian said firmly. "You can do anything."

She made a face, then unlocked her phone, tapped the screen, and held it to her ear. "Okay, I'm going to do it. Unless he doesn't pick up, then – Oh, hi, Craig. It's Rose." She looked up, eyes bulged and full of terror. "Good. How are you?" She took a deep breath. "Yes, I've had some time to think about your offer. I'd...like to give it a try."

Lucy pumped her fists in the air and Lillian sat on the couch, covering her gaping mouth with her hand.

Maybe it wasn't the most responsible scheme they'd come up with together. So what? It was the first time Rose had seemed excited in months. She needed it.

Rose ended the call a moment later and let out a squeal.

"I can't believe I'm doing this!" she yelled.

"I can't either." Lillian laughed. "You're wild!"

"Okay, getting down to business." Lucy stood, smoothing her shirt with her hands. "Grab your purse. I'm taking you shopping. My treat. You'll feel more the part if you look the part. We need to get your first day outfit. Maybe your first week of outfits. I don't know."

"You don't have to buy me anything," Rose protested.

"Now!" Lucy pointed at her. "Move it, sister. You too, Lillian. This is a girls' trip."

Lillian got up and tapped Rose on the shoulder. "You can't fight her. Just go with it."

She sighed, a small smile on her lips. "Fine."

Chapter Six

The seaplane's engine hummed along, a calming drone for Rose's nerves. She thought her last flight was a special treat – first seeing the islands from above, then a short hour later, the city of Seattle expanding beneath them, the rows of buildings surrounded by the sea.

But now this was her commute to work. It was surreal, and she couldn't get enough of the view.

The flight was too short, really. The pilot announced their approach for Lake Union and Rose gazed through her window, down at the lake littered with white boats gliding in slow motion.

As the plane got lower, details came into view: the windows on the buildings, people riding bicycles on the streets below, the yellow flags lining the docks. They touched down gently and glided to a slow, bumbling crawl. A boat with a tall, blindingly white sail drifted by, and she could see the Space Needle straight ahead.

It was the perfect day to start her new job. The sun was shining, yet the air was cool. For once, she wasn't sweating. The outfit Lucy had bought for her was like nothing she'd ever pick out for herself – an A-line black dress that went to her knee, the fabric a soft and cool wool, and a blazer that extended just beyond her hips and provided "a long line for the eye," as Lucy had put it.

She was right about everything. Rose hadn't wanted to trust her, but the outfit looked amazing. Even the blazer's loud print, with tangerine and pink flowers, looked marvelous. Rose looked like a professional, and she felt like a million bucks.

It might as well have cost a million bucks. Rose never would've picked clothes so expensive, and she fully intended to pay Lucy back once she got her first paycheck. She wasn't counting on getting many paychecks – surely they'd fire her once they found out what a fraud she was – but even a few would help. Then she'd get back on the job market, *and* she'd have this awesome outfit to show for it.

The pilot stopped the plane and hopped out. He offered Rose a hand as she stepped onto the dock in her heels.

"Lovely flying with you," he said with a nod, his eyes peeking out from behind his aviators.

Rose smiled at him. "You too!"

She walked to the street where a car was waiting. Craig had sent it; he said she could order the company car any time she was in town.

It all seemed extravagant, but what was she going to do, refuse? She had to act like it was all normal, expected, even.

The driver spotted her and waved. "Dr. Woodson, very nice to meet you."

"Please, call me Rose."

"Rose," he said with a nod. "May I take your luggage?"

She gripped the strap on her shoulder. She'd stuffed enough clothes for a week into the little duffel bag she'd borrowed from Lucy. Initially, she was proud of herself for fitting everything in, but now she was embarrassed by how rounded and messy it looked. "No, that's all right, but thank you."

"I'm happy to drop it off at your room."

"Oh." She paused. That week she'd decided to stay at one of the SerenadeMe apartments Craig had told her about. She wanted to be able to come into the office, since her first clients were going to be locals.

"It's no problem at all," he said, extending a hand. "Please, allow me."

How could she pretend like this was normal? "Are you sure?" she asked in a small voice.

He grinned. "Absolutely. It'll give me an excuse to get myself another tea. I'm doing a cleanse."

She pulled the strap off her shoulder and handed the bag to him. "Thank you. I really do appreciate it. I've done the tea cleanse – what day are you on?"

"Of course. And it's day three. I feel awful. When does it get better?"

She made a face. "Honestly? Never. I thought I was dying the entire time."

He laughed and waved a hand toward the car. Rose slipped into the SUV, where a glass bottle of bubbly water was waiting for her.

Rose didn't dare touch it. The bubbly water was where she drew the line. It looked too expensive.

The driver finished loading her bag and they were off, winding through the streets and arriving at the building a few minutes later.

"Thank you again," Rose said, opening the door before the driver had a chance to do it for her.

She stepped onto the sidewalk and looked up at the tower of glass and stone.

This was where it had all begun, except this time she wouldn't have to beg anyone to help her with the elevator. This time, she had a badge *and* a purpose.

Rose took a breath and stepped inside, the lobby bustling with people rushing to and fro.

Rose could rush, too. She picked up her pace, gliding through the gates with her badge and straight to the elevators. SerenadeMe was on the thirty-second floor, and she rode up without stopping.

When the doors opened, she stepped out and spotted Craig immediately. He stood with one arm resting on the secretary's desk.

The secretary laughed, covering her mouth, snorting.

Was he a flirt? Or just friendly?

Rose at least didn't have to worry about being hit on. She was used to being practically invisible to men, unless they wanted to talk to her boss or needed to know where to get coffee.

Maybe the blazer would make her slightly less invisible. Life could be different here. People could ask her how her weekend was, or what she wanted to get for lunch.

One could dream.

Rose smiled as she approached them. "Good morning."

"Rose!" Craig turned, grinning. "You're early. Excellent. I can give you the full tour." He leaned back and tapped the secretary's desk. "Thanks again."

She nodded. "No problem."

Craig led her around the floor – first to the gym and meditation room, then to the café with its private chef and pair of baristas, then through the HR department filled with smiling people who already knew her by name.

"I sent an email ahead of time letting people know you'd be starting," Craig said. "I hope you don't mind."

She was tickled, but she didn't want to show it. She needed to act like she expected to have such a warm welcome. "Of course not!"

Their last stop was Rose's private office.

"I apologize. It's on the smaller side," he said as he opened the door. "We can arrange for something better in the coming weeks – this was all we had time to set up on short notice."

Rose walked in. It looked like a museum. She clutched her purse close to her body, afraid of knocking anything over.

At the far end of the room was a sleek desk, the top shining white, the thin legs a rich, dark wood. A matching chair with a cushioned leather seat sat slightly askew. There was a stunning white and natural wood bookshelf sitting behind the desk and a teal velvet loveseat in the corner. Natural light poured in from the floor-to-ceiling windows, and the walls were adorned with paintings and round mirrors, all edged in gold.

"It's beautiful," she said before she could stop herself.

"You like it? Good!" He grinned. "Your computer is already set up...or it should be. Do you want to log in and I can show you a few things?"

"Sure."

Rose sunk into the plush chair. It felt even better than it looked, like it was giving her a hug.

At her old job, she'd had to scrounge a chair out of the dumpster when the wheels fell off hers. With a few repairs, she was able to use it for six years, right up until the day she was fired. She wondered who had it now.

Now was not the time to think of that, though. She pulled out the credential sheet they'd picked up in HR.

Human Resources, the keepers of secrets. They were the only people who knew her actual identity. She'd had to give them her real name and her real social security number. She had told them she went by Woodson to avoid confusion with another Rose Woodley, and they didn't bat an eye. Her name in the system was set up as Rose Woodson.

Rose took a deep breath as she began typing in her username and password. It was possible HR took the time to look her up, or to call her old school, or...

Nope. She logged right in and Craig leaned over her shoulder, pointing out the various programs.

"Obviously, I don't expect you to learn all of this today, but here's a list with a few of our elite members and how they answered their questionnaires."

"Interesting. I assume I can match them to non-elite members?"

"Yes. Those records are a bit messier, though." He pointed to an icon on the desktop. "It's all kept here, but it's the raw data. It's too much to look at. I'll have one of our developers stop by this week and get you what you need."

Rose felt a flutter in her chest. Her previous boss always needed help with wrangling large tracts of data, so much so that Rose signed up for a coding class using Python.

She'd loved it, and it had gone so well that she went to another one, and another, until she was a data wizard. Her skills were still basic – finding trends and making simple models – but it was enough at her old job.

Would it be enough here?

"I apologize, but I have to run to some meetings," Craig said, standing up. "Take your time, walk around, get to know people. I'll be back after lunch and we can chat more."

"Sounds great. Thanks, Craig."

He disappeared and she was left in the stunning silence of her magazine-perfect office.

Rose sat back and took a deep breath. She'd never been to a place like this before. When the workers saw Craig coming, they didn't hide. They waved! They seemed *happy*.

It seemed like paradise. She just needed to not mess it up.

~

It didn't take her long to get started. Despite being promised time with the developers, Rose wanted to see what she could do on her own.

She pulled up the data and started combing through it. There were millions of entries. She'd looked up a bit about SerenadeMe and knew they had around five million active users – but how many were there who had met their perfect match and disappeared? There was a lot of history, and a lot to draw from. A bunch of these people could be married by now! Have kids! White picket fences, all thanks to the app!

Half an hour into her daydreaming, her phone rang.

Without looking away from her computer, she picked it up. "Hello?"

"Rose?" The familiar voice faltered. "It's Greg."

If she hadn't been sitting down, she would've fallen over.

"Hey, hi," she said, drawing out the "hi" for four seconds. "How are you?"

"I'm good. Ah, sorry for calling you out of the blue like this. Is this weird? Am I being weird?"

Rose touched a hand to her forehead. Was today some sort of vivid dream? Had she fallen into an open manhole, and now she was hallucinating this gorgeous office and the chic outfit and the call from her ex-boyfriend who she'd been pining after since they'd broken up five years ago?

"You're always weird, Greg," she quipped.

A laugh burst out of his end of the phone. "I know, right? How are you?"

"I'm good." She paused. "Really good, actually. I started a new job today."

"That's why I'm calling. I'm not just a weirdo." He laughed again. "I saw on LinkedIn that you're working at SerenadeMe?"

Greg worked for a company in San Francisco as a data scientist. Three years ago, when she floated the idea of learning how to code, he was the one who encouraged her to do it. "You'd be great at it," he'd said. "Spreadsheets have always been your thing. This is just the next level."

In the last year, their conversations had fizzled out. Greg seemed occupied. Distant. His company was busier than ever, but they still kept in touch. They had moments like this. He noticed things, he thought about her.

Greg was her long-lost love. No one liked to hear her talk about it—they'd roll their eyes and tell her to stop dreaming, but she knew the truth. They were meant for each other. They just needed to get the timing right.

Maybe, just *maybe*, it was all coming together now?

"I'm excited for this job," she said. "It's something new."

"I've heard a lot about that company – it's incredible. Great work getting hired there. I mean, they're lucky to have you, but I think you'll like it, too."

She was glad there was no need to hide her grin. "Thanks, Greg."

"I'd love to hear more about it, and I'm going to be in Seattle in a few weeks for work. Would you want to grab dinner or something?"

Her heart thudded against her ribs. She reminded herself to act casual, as though the last time they saw each other two years ago she hadn't humiliated herself by asking him if he wanted to get back together. "Yeah, sure. That'd be nice."

"I'll text you when I'm in town and we'll figure something out."

"Okay," she said airily. "Talk to you then."

She ended the call, and after making sure it had, in fact, ended, she let out a squeal.

It could *not* get any better than this.

Well no. It could. If she could figure out how to wrangle this data on her own, how to make thoughtful, effective matches for people – she could *actually* get away with doing this job.

And if she could succeed at this job, not only would she be able to keep working at the fabulous SerenadeMe with all of its amazing perks, she would impress Greg and he'd finally admit what a fool he'd been to break up with her. They could get married at a winery like they'd always talked about, and he would tell people how he'd *almost* let her get away.

Rose sat back, cracked her fingers, and turned her eyes back to the rows upon rows of data. It was time to get to work.

Chapter Seven

His first meeting was with the developer team. It ran over time, and Craig had to quietly slip into Barney's office for his next meeting – a call with the board.

Luckily, Barney had it under control, talking through quarterly earnings and addressing the insultingly low offer an investor had made the previous week.

"They said they knew we need a cash injection and offered to pay a value equal to one time our revenue," Barney said. "I told them to come back when they got better at math."

Laughs burst through the speaker before Barney muted the phone and nodded to Craig. "I'm going to end on a high note. Anything to add?"

Craig shook his head and Barney unmuted himself. "Thanks, everyone. We'll talk next week."

He ended the call and let out a long breath.

"Rough day?" Craig asked.

"Nah, not too bad. I just still can't figure out how they could be so confident in low-balling us." He shook his head. "It's been bugging me all week."

"What company doesn't need cash?" Craig shrugged. "Don't worry about it. We've got a buyer."

Barney scoffed. "Do you mean Brett? From AptMatch?"

"I don't know why you're saying it like that, but yes. Brett."

"Because he's not serious. He's playing with us, trying to get his name in the papers to get attention and funding for his terrible app. He's a dinosaur. He doesn't know the market."

Craig wouldn't claim to be sure of Brett's intentions, but he didn't think it was that simple. "He's not a dinosaur. He's experienced, and AptMatch has twice as many users as SerenadeMe."

Barney sighed. "Yeah, because our users actually find someone and stop using the app. We're too good, Craig."

"Always have been."

"Do we even want to sell to this guy?" Barney grabbed a paperweight from his desk and rolled it between his hands. "Maybe we want to stay on. Find more growth."

Craig raised an eyebrow. "Two weeks ago, you told me you were so burnt out that you were going to sell all your possessions and float away on a catamaran."

Barney set the paperweight down. "It does sound nice, doesn't it?"

Craig laughed. He didn't disagree. Floating away from their problems was easier than facing them.

It was true their app was too good. The average user only used it for four months. They wanted to figure out why, so they'd sent out surveys with gift card raffles. Eighty percent of the respondents said they'd found a partner and they were happy.

Eighty percent!

They couldn't give up on SerenadeMe yet. They'd expanded a bit quickly and were short on cash, yes, but the company was good. The technology was remarkable. The people were top-notch.

But the two of them were falling apart. Barney was on the brink of a mental breakdown, and Craig had to take over handling a lot of the day-to-day issues. He tried to act like he had everything under control, but the truth was, he had no idea what he was doing.

Craig could design the app, and he could endlessly tweak it for better results, but he couldn't run a company. He was a fraud, through and through, and if they didn't sell soon, someone was bound to find out. Visions of users quitting *en masse* and sending the stock price plummeting kept him up at night.

The pressure was killing him, but he couldn't let the company down. They had to find a way to sell before it all fell apart.

"We're figuring it out," Craig said confidently. "The board thinks it's a good move, and I'm pretty sure I know how to get Brett to close the deal."

A smile spread across Barney's face. "Oh yeah, your matchmaker started today! What's her name again?"

"Rose." He sat back, looking up at the ceiling. "I'm telling you, she's got that something. I don't know what it is, but I have a good feeling."

Barney stood and put his suit jacket on. "The last time you had a good feeling, we ended up hiking Mount Rainier in the middle of a snowstorm."

"You're the one who made me go hiking in the first place," Craig said. "I was just trying to get it over with."

He laughed. "Yeah, sure. As long as your matchmaker doesn't almost kill us, it'll still be better than that."

"I think we're safe there."

He nodded. "I've got to run. Let me know how it's going."

"Will do."

Craig waved him off, then got up to make his way back to Rose's office.

She wasn't the answer to *all* of their problems, but the idea of a matchmaker was brilliant. It would set them apart. Pull people in. Prevent them from running this company into the ground because they were two inexperienced, overgrown college kids.

On top of that, Rose was a professional. She walked into the office this morning and she just *fit*. She greeted everyone like they were old friends and chatted with such ease. Rose had the charm of a celebrity, and that was exactly what they needed in a matchmaker.

Craig's intentions were strictly professional, but he couldn't help but notice how beautiful she was, too. If he weren't her boss, he never would've approached her.

Beautiful women were wasted on him. For one, he was too shy to talk to them, and even if he did, he couldn't get them to stick around. Craig was too quiet, too private. He'd always been this way, and the more enchanting the woman, the more closed-off he became.

It was partially why he made the app. He never dreamed his silly idea would work for people. It was wonderful, really. Someone could meet the love of their life, their partner, their soulmate – and all they had to do was take a chance and answer a few questions.

He didn't get relationships, but he could still see the beauty in it. Rose saw it, too. Maybe that was what made her so easy to talk to.

~

He knocked on her office door and she called out, "Come in!"

He walked in and it looked like she hadn't moved since he'd left, except to cover the surface of her desk with sheets of scribbled-on paper.

"Did you get lunch?" he asked.

She shook her head. "Not yet. I was trying to get this model running."

He took a step toward her. "What model?"

Rose sat back, a grin on her face. "I'm guessing your developers already made something like this, but I found the matchmaking data and tried to get some insights. I was so, *so* excited when I saw that some users reported back how long their matched relationships lasted."

"Oh yeah. That's a newer feature; we haven't really done anything with it yet."

She clapped her hands together. "*Yes!* I thought it might be new, because only about twenty percent of non-active members reported back. Anyway, I used that to build a model to figure out which questions were most influential in predicting a successful match."

Craig's mouth dropped open. "You did *what?*"

She cleared her throat. "I'm sorry, was I not supposed to – "

"No, it's – that's wonderful." He leaned in, scanning her screen. "I'm amazed, actually. And a little bit annoyed no one else has thought of doing this yet."

She laughed. "It's hard when there's so much data. Sometimes you need a fresh set of eyes."

Craig couldn't stop smiling. Barney had nothing to worry about. Rose was amazing. She was the *key* to everything. "You're right. Sometimes a little attention is all you need."

Chapter Eight

Without meaning to, Rose stayed late on her first day. It wasn't *entirely* her fault. Though her new model was more complicated than initially expected, her concentration kept getting interrupted by visitors.

No fewer than a dozen people stopped in to introduce themselves, one even bringing welcome cupcakes, but Rose couldn't chat for long. She was a woman on a mission.

By seven that evening, however, she had to pause that mission. Her computer screen was filled with errors and her eyes were having a hard time focusing.

She left the office and got dinner on her walk back to the company-sponsored apartment. The building was only a block away from the office, and as Craig had said, it wasn't anything fancy – a small studio with a kitchen in the corner – but it was clean, and after a long day, it felt like home.

Rose was just settling onto the couch with her burrito bowl when a video call lit up on her phone.

Lucy!

She smiled and answered it. "Hey."

"Hey, girl, hey!" Lucy yelled.

"We miss you!" Lillian said, pushing in.

Rose laughed. "I miss you too."

"How was your first day?"

Rose puffed out her cheeks. "Amazing. Terrifying. And tiring."

Lillian leaned closer. "Did you say terrifying?"

"Must've been the flight." Lucy shook her head knowingly.

Though her sister had confronted her fear of flying, she hadn't exactly conquered it. "No, the flight was beautiful. It's terrifying because everyone is so nice and welcoming and helpful."

Lucy cocked her head to the side. "I'm sorry, what? Why are you scared, then?"

"She's scared of messing it up," Lillian said.

Exactly. Rose hardly had to explain things to Lillian. "I know I'm not qualified for this job but...I feel like I can still do *something* cool here. They have all this data on users, and today I found information on who matched and how long they dated. It's really fascinating!"

"No one is qualified for this job," Lillian said, "because no one *could* be qualified. It's a made-up job."

"Yeah," Lucy added. "It's not like there's a matchmaker school churning out new grads." She paused. "At least I don't think there is one. If so, I should look into enrolling."

"Lucy, no." Lillian held up a hand. "You don't need to go to any more schools, and this isn't about you. Rose! Tell us all about your day."

Rose took a deep breath and started talking. She hadn't wanted to babble as long as she did, but there was so much to tell – the car that came to get her, her fancy office, the office birthday cupcakes Cassie (or was it Cassandra?) from customer service made that morning.

She had to tell them all of that before she could get to the most incredible part of the story. "And, after all of that, you won't believe who called me."

Lillian spoke first. "That guy who interviewed you last week who was super rude? Did he offer you a job?"

Rose shook her head. "Not him. Someone good."

Lucy groaned. "Was it Greg?"

"Yes!" Rose's smile faded. "Why did you say his name like that?"

"Because it's *just* like him to rise from his murky bog to drag you down."

"He doesn't live in a murky bog," Rose snapped. "And he's not dragging me down. He saw I got a new job and congratulated me. He wants to get dinner soon! It's *finally* happening! The timing is perfect. I can feel it."

Lucy and Lillian looked at each other, then back at Rose.

"What? Don't make those faces," Rose said. "If Lillian can get back with her high school boyfriend, why can't I get back with my college boyfriend?"

"Dustin is a different story," Lucy said. "He's not a jerk."

Rose narrowed her eyes. "Greg isn't a jerk. We've just been...we have a complicated history. Back me up, Lillian."

Lillian bit her lip. "It *is* complicated."

"No, it isn't." Lucy rolled her eyes. "It's not complicated at all. It's actually *very* simple. He had the chance to be with you for the last five years, and he chose not to be." She crossed her arms. "There. That's all the history you need."

It was so like Lucy to try to oversimplify things. How could she understand? Rose and Greg were like two ships passing in the night, and then passing each other again and again. The dock was always full, or a storm blew in, or one of them had to really commit to work for a while.

They had something special, though, and she never stopped thinking about or dreaming of him. No other guy measured up. He was *the one*, she just knew it. It was tragic, it was torturous, but it was *romantic*.

What did Lucy know about romance?

"He always leaves you upset," Lillian said gently.

Rose shook her head. "That was just that one time, and it was my fault. He wasn't in the place for a relationship, and I shouldn't have brought it up."

Lucy took control of the phone. "Listen. I need to tell you something. I think you deserve to know."

Another story about Greg as the creature from the San Francisco lagoon? "Okay, what?"

"Greg is engaged."

The couch Rose was sitting on started to spin. She put a hand out and sat up. "What? No, he's not."

She nodded. "He is. I wasn't going to tell you because I thought he'd finally disappeared for good, but..." She sighed. "A friend of mine has a catering company and said she met with this really rich family who made a big deal about sparing no expense for a wedding. Long story short, it was Greg and his fiancée. Her family owns a cell phone company or something."

"A cell phone company?" Rose shook her head. "And she's a horrible bridezilla monster and I need to rescue him?"

Lucy winced. "Apparently, she's really nice. *Sweet as honey* is what my friend said."

Rose had to unclench her jaw. "You're telling me Greg is marrying some telecom heiress? And she's *nice?*"

It made no sense. Greg hated being around rich people. It always ruined his career prospects in Silicon Valley. He'd say the wrong thing to the wrong person and end up fired. It had happened three times in the last five years. He was a total dunce.

Rose loved him for it.

Lillian took the phone back. "I know this is hard to hear, and I'm sorry, but maybe it's for the best?"

Maybe it was, if Greg was coming to see her because this engagement felt wrong.

He was a guy who couldn't make up his mind about *anything.* He used to make them late to things because he couldn't decide which color t-shirt to wear.

He'd been telling her for years it wasn't the right time for them, and now this? An engagement? To his sworn enemy?

He had to be losing his mind in panic. This was not a man who could commit, and there was no way their dinner was a coincidence. He was realizing he was making a mistake, and he was coming to fix it.

She couldn't say that to her sisters, though. They'd think she was out of her mind, imagining things that weren't there.

It wasn't for them to understand. She knew Greg, and he knew her. He'd see what a success she was at this job, he'd finally see that he'd waited too long, and it would all work out. Her life was changing. *She* was changing.

She'd keep it to herself for now. "Yes, maybe it is for the best," Rose said, happy for the conversation to drift to another topic.

~

The rest of her week went off without a hitch. Rose went into the office early Tuesday morning, and with fresh eyes, she was able to fix the errors in her model.

On Wednesday, she met with a lead data scientist who helped her understand some of the legacy data, and on Thursday, her model could spit out a list of potential questions and matches in under thirty seconds.

The only problem was she couldn't find anything about her first client. She had his name, but there were no questionnaires or stats in his profile. Rose requested a meeting with Craig to discuss it, and to her surprise, he dropped by that afternoon.

"Knock knock," he said, popping his head into her office.

"Oh, hey!" Rose tidied a stack of papers on her desk. "Thanks for coming."

He took a seat across from her. "Of course. How's it going? I'm sorry I've been so busy. The investor has us running around like fools."

"No problem at all. I've been working on my model and wanted to get started with my first client. I can't seem to get into his file. It's Seymour Wilkins, right?"

"Ah." Craig nodded. "Our elite members are password protected. I'll message Lydia to give you access."

"Thanks. I was thinking I'd set up a video call with him on Monday to get to know him."

Craig frowned. "Next week? My schedule is pretty booked."

"Oh." Rose sat back. "I didn't realize you'd want to be involved."

"Well, you know, if you wanted the extra support, I wanted to offer it."

Hm. If she was going to compete with a telecom heiress, Rose needed to play the role. She wasn't scared little Rose Woodley anymore. She was Rose Woodson, PhD, with a hot shot tech job and a glut of matchmaking data at her fingertips.

She sat up straight and the strangest thing came out of her mouth. "Don't you trust me, Craig?"

He laughed and put his hands up. "You're right. I'm being a control freak. I do that sometimes; it's no reflection of you. Obviously, you know what you're doing."

Obviously.

At least Rose could pretend she knew what she was doing, and wasn't that the only thing that mattered?

"Thanks, boss. That means a lot."

She'd fake it until she made it, and she had the weekend to figure out her next moves.

Chapter Nine

Per Rose's request, Lillian reported to The Grand Madrona Hotel on Saturday morning for brunch. Rose's text stated she needed to discuss "important matchmaking business" and told them to "bring the menfolk."

Luckily, Dustin had the day off. He picked up both Lillian and Lucy, and they made their way to the hotel.

"Is this like when the mafia has a meeting of the seven families?" Lucy mused as they pulled into the hotel's parking lot.

"Exactly like that," Dustin said. "Except the seven families thing was from *Game of Thrones*, and this is only your family, and none of you are in the mafia. I think."

Lillian laughed. She still couldn't get over how lucky she was to be with him, and living on Orcas Island made it feel all the more magical. The hiking, the sunsets on the water, the oyster shucking – it was like something out of a dream, so much so that sometimes she thought it *was* a dream. Two nights prior, she'd awakened with a start and remembered, all of a sudden, that they were together, he was real, and he was *hers*.

She had fallen back to sleep with a grin on her face.

They got to the hotel and went straight to the in-house restaurant. Lillian's mom Claire was already chatting with her cousin Marty and his girlfriend Emma.

Marty waved a hello as they approached. "We can't stay long. We have a hike planned."

He looked at his watch, then darted his hand into his pocket.

"We can stay for a bit." Emma looked at him and gently touched his shoulder. "There's no rush, is there?"

Marty took his hand out of his pocket, then zipped it shut. "No, it might rain later and that'll ruin it. We should really get going."

"It won't ruin anything!" Emma said brightly. "I packed my rain jacket."

"That's good." Marty scratched his head. "Still, we can't stay long."

Lillian wasn't used to seeing him look so agitated. What had gotten into him?

Before she could ask what was wrong, Rose walked in, a bag slung over her shoulder and a grin on her face. "Hey every-one!" she yelled from across the room.

She'd come straight off the plane from Seattle. When Lillian had heard that was Rose's plan, she'd worried that perhaps this new job was working her too hard and she'd fallen into old patterns.

But Rose looked anything but overworked. Her hair was straightened, her makeup was done, and she was wearing the cute velour jumpsuit Lucy had insisted on buying for her.

"Dr. Woodson!" Lucy said, pulling her in for a hug. "Rob couldn't make it because he's on a business trip, but I'm confident I can speak for us both."

"I'm sure you can," Rose said.

Their mom stepped in and hugged her next. "Dr. Woodson?" she asked. "What's that about?"

Lillian bit her lip. Her mom wouldn't approve of the lie they'd come up with. She knew about the job, of course, but not *how* Rose had gotten it. It was best not to dwell on the topic. "It's just a joke we have," Lillian said, giving Rose a side hug.

"Yeah," Lucy added. "Because Rose only got this job after her new boss confused her for a doctor of psychology named Dr. Woodson. Isn't that funny?"

Lillian shut her eyes. So much for keeping it quiet.

A scowl formed on her mom's face. "What? You're pretending to be someone else?"

"Don't worry about it, Mom," Rose said, waving a hand. "I've got everything under control."

Lillian had to turn her head so they wouldn't see her smile. This was certainly not the beaten-down version of Rose who'd arrived on the island a month ago.

In fact, she was starting to sound a bit like Lucy – perhaps because of the job? The jumpsuit?

Whatever it was, it was dangerous. And fascinating.

"It's really nice to see you all," Marty said, "but can we please be excused?"

"*Marty!*" Emma elbowed his side. "What's gotten into you? We can stay for a bit. Don't be rude!"

He let out a sigh and looked at his watch. "I don't know. The rain could be bad, and it's going to get busy if we wait too long..."

Rose turned to him. "Why are you so sweaty? Are you okay?"

Emma looked him up and down. "If you're not feeling well, we don't have to do this hike."

"I feel fine." He unzipped his pocket again. "I'm dressed for the hike. It's hot in here. That's all."

Lillian tried to catch Rose's eye, but she was watching Marty.

She spoke again. "No, it's okay. You can go, but first tell me one thing."

Marty nodded. "Anything."

"How'd you both know you'd found the right partner?"

Marty crossed his arms. "Why are you asking that?"

"Oh, is *that* all you need to know?" Emma laughed. "It's hard to put into words." She paused, looking up at Marty with a bemused smile. "I can tell you he's a wonderful person, and that made it easy. But before I met him, I felt like..." Her voice trailed off. "This is kind of pathetic, but I felt like a burden. Like no one actually wanted to be with me."

"That's *so* not true," Marty said, turning to her. "Your ex was a terrible person, and that was the problem. You could never be a burden."

Emma smiled and dropped her eyes. "See? The sweetest."

"I'm not sweet." He shook his head. "*You're* the sweet one, and you're way too nice."

"Ugh!" Lucy put her hand up. "Take your overly sweet butts hiking before you make me sick."

Marty laughed and put his arm around Emma. "Thank you!"

Lillian felt Dustin grab her hand and she glanced up at him. He winked and butterflies took off in her stomach.

Rose waited until they were gone to speak again. "I didn't realize Marty was proposing to Emma today. I wouldn't have asked them to come."

"What?" Lucy blurted out. "How do you know he's proposing to her?"

Her mom gasped. "Do you really think so? That's so wonderful."

"Isn't it obvious?" Rose shrugged. "He's being weird, he kept putting his hand in his pocket, and he's worried about the time. Marty is *never* worried about being on time. You can basically distract him at any moment with a piece of cake."

Lillian frowned. "You have a point."

"Why don't we follow them on the hike so we can all enjoy the moment together?" Dustin suggested. "Jump out and yell *surprise* when she says yes?"

Everyone laughed and took their seats at the table. Lillian wasn't shocked Rose was the only one who knew what was going on with Marty. She picked up on everything – except when it came to her own relationships. There she was blinded, especially when it came to Greg.

Oh, Greg. Lillian didn't hate the man. It wasn't that simple. When he and Rose were together, it was fine. Rose was happy. She'd thought she'd found *The One*, that they'd graduate and get married and have a family.

Greg couldn't see it, though, and any talks of the future scared him. When Rose had started asking questions about where things were going, he broke up with her in a panic. From then on, he refused to fully cut ties, instead insisting they were still friends.

Let's stay friends is one of the cruelest sentences in the English language. What good is friendship after a life-altering love? It's the hollow chocolate Easter bunny of relationships.

Rose didn't need him to be her friend. She needed him to make up his mind whether he wanted to be with her or not.

But Greg couldn't make up his mind. He couldn't decide if they should be long distance, then he couldn't decide if they should date once she moved to San Francisco, and *then* he couldn't decide if he was the marrying type at all.

He'd pulled poor Rose along for years, promising her this and that. It wasn't malicious, but it was exceptionally self-absorbed. It was always *what does Greg want, what does Greg need?*

It was the one thing Rose couldn't see. Her nature was to set herself on fire to keep others warm, and Greg was happy to keep her nearby.

Lillian's hope was that maybe, just *maybe*, this job would help her see the light.

Rose pulled out a notebook and a pink pen. "Thank you all for coming here today. Mom, is Chip busy?"

She shook her head. "He's on his way. Just dealing with some hotel business."

"Good." Rose clicked her pen. "Since I'm going to start my formal matchmaking services next week, I thought it would be wise to talk to some actual couples about how they met, the challenges they had, and how they knew they'd found the right person."

Lucy held up a hand. "I'll go first. Before me, Rob kept dating the wrong kind of girl."

"What was wrong with them?" asked Dustin. "Other than not being you."

"The 'not me' part was a big problem," Lucy said solemnly, "but really, he just took whoever showed up. He was too focused on his job to put effort into anything else."

Rose scribbled on the notepad. "Why was he so focused on his job?"

Lucy sighed, looking up wistfully. "He was trying to live up to expectations set by his dad. I don't think he realized he was doing it half the time, but almost everything he did was for his dad's approval. He was afraid to think about what kind of life *he* wanted, but once he did, he realized he had the perfect woman right in front of him."

Lillian chortled a laugh. "The perfect woman?"

"I'm just repeating the man's own words," Lucy snapped. "It took him forever to find me."

"I see." Rose finished writing and looked up. "And what about you? Why did it take you so long to find him?"

Lucy crossed her arms over her chest. "What do you mean *so long*? I'm young. It didn't take me *so long*."

Lillian stifled a laugh. Time to referee. "There's no need to get defensive. It's no secret that your relationships before Rob were... not ideal."

"I had bad luck! It wasn't my fault."

"Would it be fair to say," Lillian said slowly, "that you were afraid of being in love, *really* in love, and losing that person, so you avoided and sabotaged and ran from things?"

Lucy stared at the table, her lips pursed, until finally she let out a breath. "Maybe."

Rose laughed. "Am I allowed to write that down?"

"That's life," their mom said, cutting in. "No one is perfect. We have to figure things out as we go along."

Just then, Chip walked into the restaurant and spotted them at the table. A smile spread across his face and he walked over. "Hey kids. Hey, Honey."

"Well, if it isn't our not-so-evil stepfather," Lucy said. "Chip, why would you say it took me so long to find a boyfriend?"

He didn't hesitate to answer. "Because you're scary."

The table erupted into laughter, with even Lucy joining in. "I like that." She grinned. "I like being scary."

"Mom," Rose said, turning her attention, "why did it take *you* so long to find a boyfriend – now husband – and why was it Lucy's fault?"

Everyone laughed again except for their mom.

She answered with sincerity. "It wasn't Lucy's fault; it wasn't anyone's fault. Romance didn't cross my mind until all of you were grown up. I didn't have time to date. I was too busy."

Lillian reached across the table and put a hand on her shoulder. "I'm sorry, Mom."

"Why are you sorry?" She patted her hand and smiled warmly. "It all worked out. I got to spend many happy years raising you girls, and when you were ready to go out on your own, I met Chip. What could be more perfect than that?"

Chip locked eyes with her and they smiled.

Lucy snapped her fingers. "Focus, newlyweds, *focus*! And no kissing." Lucy shook her head. "Chip, what's your story?"

He frowned. "What do you mean?"

Rose cut in. "How'd you know Mom was the one for you?"

"That's a big question. Whew." He rubbed his chin with his hand. "I've never thought about it. I just knew."

"Not helpful," Lucy said.

Chip shrugged, grinning. "I had to stop being stubborn to see her in front of me."

Lillian looked at Rose – she was diligently writing this all down.

Dustin cleared his throat. "I feel like I should be excused from this because I knew Lillian was the perfect girl for me and tried to get her to marry me in high school, but she had to go and be all reasonable about it and tell me *no*."

Lillian laughed. "It wasn't the right time. We both needed to grow up."

"But how'd you know he was the one for you now?" asked Rose.

Lillian needed to tread carefully, because Rose had already tried comparing Greg to Dustin, and they were *nothing* alike. "I had a lot of soul-searching to do. I was insecure, and I had accepted less from a partner than I should have."

"Why were you insecure?" Lucy said, shaking her head. "You're awesome."

"It doesn't work like that." Lillian glanced at Rose, who was still writing.

They both had their issues with insecurity – issues that escaped Lucy.

Lillian continued. "Still, I was in love with Dustin, but I truly believed he wanted nothing to do with me."

"*Babe!*" Dustin put his arm around her. "I've always been crazy about you."

She smiled. "That's the thing. I know that now. It's not..." Lillian paused, gathering her thoughts. How could she make sure Rose didn't twist her words to assure herself about Greg? It wasn't the same situation, as much as Rose wanted it to be.

"People have to be able to change," Lillian finally said. "They have to *want* to change, they have to want to see their problems and make sure they're not hurting the ones who love them."

Rose stopped writing and set her pen down. "We should probably order." She picked up a menu. "Is that blueberry French toast still on special?"

Uh oh. Rose had gotten her message, loud and clear.

Lillian shot Dustin a look, and he patted her leg under the table.

"I know what you were trying to say," he said in a low voice. "Maybe she's not ready to hear it yet."

"I guess not." Lillian sighed. "She shuts down anytime I even hint at talking about Greg."

He squeezed her hand. "Don't worry. I think she's figuring things out."

Rose pointed at Lucy. "Oh! I wanted to tell you. The pilot from my flight this morning told me my outfit was 'glamorous'!"

"It is," Lucy said simply. "He was probably hitting on you."

Rose laughed. "Yeah, right."

Lillian looked at Dustin. He was smiling to himself. Maybe he was right.

Oh, how she hoped he was right.

Chapter Ten

Though the matchmaker brunch was less insightful than Rose hoped it would be, it was still fun. By the end, her face hurt from laughing, and just before they left, Marty sent a text that read, "She said yes!!!" complete with a smiling picture of the happy couple atop Mt. Constitution.

Back home, Rose went over her notes and tried to see if there were any hidden clues to all those happy relationships.

What she found surprised her. As different as everyone's stories were, they all had something in common: fear.

In one form or another, fear held everyone back – fear of loss, fear of their own insecurities, fear of not meeting expectations.

Even Lucy, whom Chip correctly characterized as scary, seemed fearless – but she wasn't. She'd been afraid of being hurt and she ran from love at every chance. In the end, even scary Lucy was only human.

Rose spent the weekend pouring over books on the science behind long-lasting relationships, desperate to learn as much as she could before returning to work. Her first was the one she'd supposedly written, and she branched out from there.

Though Craig wasn't rushing her, Rose was eager to get started. She needed to prove her worth – both to the company and to herself.

On Monday, she decided to send a message to her first client, Seymour, through the SerenadeMe app.

He answered within an hour. "Can't wait to work with you. I'm free to chat on Friday. Anytime!"

Rose gasped when she saw his message. Then she sat frozen, staring at her screen.

This was happening, and she really had to sell it. If she wasn't ready, she had to find a way to look ready. Channel her inner Lucy, call up whatever courage she had, and fake it.

She took a deep breath, straightened her shoulders, and set up a video call with him on Friday. For the rest of the week, she combed through his profile and the preliminary matches selected by the SerenadeMe software.

From her first impression, it seemed like Seymour was a great catch. He was twenty-five, which, thinking of it, made her feel old. Why was everyone suddenly younger than she was?

No matter. That wasn't the focus right now. The focus was Seymour, a videogame developer living in Seattle. He loved to cook, he loved both cats *and* dogs, and he had cute-looking pictures in his profile.

Rose didn't see any red flags. It was unnerving. What could she possibly do to help him?

By the time their meeting rolled around, Rose had all but memorized his answers to the 126 matchmaking questions. She told herself she was as prepared as possible, but her traitorous heart still thundered in her chest as she logged onto the call.

Her face popping onto the screen distracted her for a moment. She couldn't believe how professional she looked. Her office was so pretty and serene that it almost looked fake.

She forced a smile. She could do this. Rose Woodson could do this.

Within seconds, Seymour popped onto her screen and waved. "Hi!"

He looked similar to his pictures – slim, with curly dark brown hair, brown eyes, and a brief flash of a smile. A cute young man, as far as she could tell.

Young man. She shook her head. If Lucy heard her say something like that, she'd call her an old maid.

"It's nice to meet you. I'm Rose, the matchmaker at SerenadeMe."

"It's really nice to meet you, Rose." He paused. "I'm going to be honest—I'm super nervous about this."

If only he knew. "You have no reason to be, but I totally get that. It's a scary thing, dating, isn't it?"

He nodded. "Petrifying."

"I can assure you that you're in good hands," she lied. "Why don't you tell me why you decided to sign up for the personal matchmaker service?"

He took a deep breath and nodded. "Sure, yeah. Okay, so, my last relationship was, uh..." He stopped. "Can I start over?"

Rose laughed. "Of course. Listen. To tell you the truth, I'm a little nervous myself."

He cocked his head to the side. "Why?"

"I've been looking at your profile, and from what I can see, you're a catch. I've been trying to figure out why you need me, and I'm afraid it's because you're going to say you only date supermodels or something."

A laugh burst out of him. "No! It's nothing like that."

Rose ran a hand over her forehead. "Phew."

"I signed up because I'm terrible at dating. I hate going to bars, I'm awkward when I message people on apps...I'm just bad at it."

He told her about his romantic history – not that there was much to tell. He'd had two previous relationships, and one hardly counted because it was the sister of a friend who strung him along whenever she broke up with her boyfriend.

Beyond that, there were a slew of first dates where Seymour shrunk more into himself after each one.

Forty minutes into their conversation, Rose decided to push him a bit. "Let me ask you a few questions. Are you looking for a serious relationship?"

He nodded eagerly. "Absolutely. I want someone to share my life with."

Okay, that was good. She could work with that. "I want you to stop for a second. Don't answer right away. Why haven't you found that person yet?"

He looked down and shrugged. "I guess because I haven't met her yet?"

Rose stared at him. "Why?"

He looked down and rubbed his forehead. "I'm really shy, and – I don't know. I just don't feel like anyone would want to date me. I think I give up too easily."

There it was – fear! "Why don't you think anyone would want to date you?"

He smiled and rolled his eyes. "I'm a nerd who loves video games and dresses like a dork."

Nothing could be further from the truth. Rose had to stop her jaw from dropping open.

"Seymour – I mean this in the most platonic way possible – you are a total cutie."

He scratched his head, squinting up at her. "Thanks."

She went on. "I mean it. And I don't think you dress like a dork, but a new outfit could really boost your confidence."

"I wouldn't even know where to start. I buy all my clothes from Target."

There was nothing wrong with Target, but even in the grainy video, she could tell his t-shirt was three sizes too big. "It's not about designer clothes or spending a lot of money." She paused. "How would you feel about meeting with me and sprucing up your wardrobe? It won't change who you are, but it might make you feel a little more confident. What do you think?"

"Are you serious?"

Was she serious? She didn't know why she'd blurted that out. It probably crossed some professional boundary. In fact, it was an unflinchingly *weird* thing to offer.

But she felt bad for the kid – er, guy. She wanted to help him, and her experience getting clothes with Lucy had really boosted her own confidence.

"Of course I'm serious! I'd love to help you!"

"That would be *amazing*. Really. I'm free all weekend."

"How about today? At five?" Rose asked. "I'll personally make sure you meet your match feeling like a million bucks."

Seymour grinned from ear to ear. "I'm in."

Chapter Eleven

T hings with AptMatch were speeding up. Craig met with Brett three times that week, answering questions and talking numbers. He always insisted on coming into the office with an entourage ten people deep. Craig wondered if it was some sort of flex, if he was trying to intimidate them.

It didn't take much to intimidate Craig, but he knew better than to show it.

Their last conversation kept edging closer to proprietary information Brett clearly thought Craig would let slip. Instead, he changed the topic, telling him about Rose and the new matchmaking service.

"People are going to go crazy for this," Brett said, tipping his ten-gallon hat. "Just you wait."

Craig couldn't figure out why Brett dressed like that. He wasn't a cowboy. He'd grown up in Connecticut, but wore that hat and pointed boots like a uniform, and talked with a slight drawl.

"They're *already* going crazy for it," Barney said, taking the lead. "We're charging ten thousand per consult, and within a week, we've had more than three hundred applications."

Brett leaned in, a toothpick hanging off his lip. "Is that right?" Craig could almost see the dollar signs in his eyes.

"It's a good problem for a company," Barney said casually, his voice lightly mirroring Brett's drawl. "We either have to hire more matchmakers, or we need to increase the price."

A smile spread across Brett's face. "Why not both?" He chuckled, sitting back and patting his stomach. "You boys know I've been working on my final offer. I'll have it to you next month and I'm confident everyone'll be happy."

Craig glanced at Barney and suppressed a smile. It was clear that ol' Brett was worried they'd sell to someone else.

Good. The sooner this deal was done, the better. He'd be able to breathe again and wouldn't have to wake up at night in a cold sweat, panicked the company was going to come crashing down around him.

Craig had never imagined himself as the head of a company. He'd never wanted people to count on him. He'd just wanted to make a dating app. It had gotten out of hand so quickly.

Barney, ever a pro, gave nothing away. "We look forward to seeing your final offer."

He stood and Brett followed his lead, offering handshakes all around. "Take care, fellas."

Brett left the conference room, the members of his staff spotting him in the hallway and swarming around like he was a queen bee.

Alone again, Barney spoke. "I have to hand it to you. I didn't see this coming."

Craig shrugged. "I know, but I think he's serious."

Barney shook his head. "It's not just that. It's all this interest in our new resident matchmaker. People are falling over themselves to meet with her."

Craig kept his eyes down. He wasn't the only one charmed by her. "I know."

"Is she going to be able to deliver?"

"Of course. Yeah." He nodded. "I mean, I think so."

He patted Craig on the shoulder. "I have no choice but to believe in you."

Craig laughed. "Thanks, man."

"I've got meetings all week." His eyes drifted to the window and his stare fixed on a distant spot. "Supposed to be good weather for sailing, though."

"Barney," Craig said slowly, "you can't float away yet. We need to make a graceful exit."

Barney let out a grunt, still staring.

"We can't let things fall apart. We're *so* close, and our employees don't know we're losing our minds. They count on us. They need their jobs intact when we leave."

"You're right." Barney took a deep breath and turned back to face him. "I don't know how we got this far, man."

"Me either."

He took a swig from the mug on his desk and shook his head. "All right. Meetings."

~

After catching a reporter from the Seattle Ledger sniffing around the office, Craig sent Rose back to Orcas Island for the week. He didn't want publicity about their new program getting out, and he didn't want to put too much pressure on Rose.

Still, everyone and their mother seemed to know about her existence, and he needed to see how she was doing. He decided to take the trip to the island and spend some time working with her. It was the perfect excuse to get away for a few days, and it gave him a chance to finish up some tasks at the house he was renovating for his parents.

That afternoon, he caught a flight and met with his electrician for a final inspection. As he'd hoped, everything checked out, and after a short hour, he was left alone in the large, quiet house.

He'd picked a place on the west side of the island and blown out the walls to make space for enormous windows overlooking the water. The sunsets were breathtaking, and he'd tried to anticipate every little detail to make the house perfect.

A year in, perfection was still out of reach. He was running out of money, though, and his parents had recently mentioned plans to find "a nice place to settle down" for retirement.

It was time to show them the house. Once he got the profits from selling SerenadeMe, he could finish up the last details, maybe even buy a place to live himself.

It would work out. They would pull it off. They had to.

He took a deep breath and walked toward the ocean-view window, his footsteps echoing in the empty room.

It was quiet, almost eerily so. A sailboat meandered into view and he stared at it, the stark white hull slicing through the endless blue waves.

He watched, mesmerized, until the spell was broken by his phone ringing.

It was Lydia. "Hey. Is everything all right?"

"Everything is great," she said. "Rose's first review just rolled in."

His heartbeat quickened. "Yeah?"

"The client said he would give Rose a hundred stars if he could. She was extremely personable, knowledgeable, and kind, and he said his match was perfect. He says he's never felt a connection like this before, and he just wanted to send this review before deleting the app."

"This was her *first* client?" Craig hadn't even known she was going to meet with anyone.

"Yeah! I sent it to her in an email and she responded right away. Seems like she's really excited, too."

He should feel happy, but all he felt was a fluttering panic. He had far less control of this entire matchmaker scheme than he needed to. Things could spiral. "This is great," he lied. "Thanks, Lydia."

He hung up and called Rose, who thankfully answered after two rings.

"Hello, you've got Rose."

"Hey, it's Craig. I heard you got a rave review from your first matchmaking client."

"Yes! I can't believe it." She paused. "I mean, I hoped it would go well, but I didn't expect it to go *this* well."

"I can't tell you how welcome this news is." He cleared his throat. "Should we celebrate? Talk next steps? I'm on the island; we could grab dinner."

As soon as he said it, he regretted it. Rose was a beautiful woman. What if she thought he was trying to hit on her by suggesting dinner like that?

But Rose didn't miss a beat. "Yes! I would love to talk to you about what I'm thinking for the next clients."

A weight lifted off his chest. "Great."

"I've been dying to get pizza," she added. "There's this place in Deer Harbor overlooking the water that's calling my name."

"I love pizza. How about seven o'clock?"

"I'll see you there!"

He put his phone back into his pocket and looked at the water. The sailboat had faded into a dot on the horizon, and another had floated into view.

Thankfully Rose hadn't thought anything of him suggesting dinner, and in truth, it wasn't an odd thing for him to do. He took other employees to dinner all the time. Sometimes they'd skip out of work early and hash out ideas over food and drinks.

Why did it feel different now?

He shifted his feet and turned away from the window. There was an obvious reason he wasn't ready to admit to himself, so instead he told himself it was because Rose was so important for the company.

Yeah, that was all.

~

Craig got to the restaurant early and was seated at a table near the window overlooking the parking lot.

At least it wasn't romantic.

Rose arrived right on time, waving as she approached.

"Thanks for coming." He stood and was about to pull out her chair before stopping himself mid-action.

That seemed inappropriate, didn't it? He shouldn't try so hard. He was her *boss,* not her prince charming. She could pull out her own chair.

She didn't seem to notice his awkward hand movements. "The pleasure is all mine. I'm *so* excited for this. I've been resisting getting pizza for the last two weeks. I've been trying to watch my diet."

He took his seat. "Some weeks pizza makes up the entirety of my diet."

"Men." Rose shook her head. "You can get away with eating garbage and still look great."

Did she just say he looked great? His heart leapt and he opened his mouth to respond. "Uh..."

She laughed and put a hand over her mouth. "I'm sorry. I'm not judging how you look. Or minimizing your struggles with weight if you have them. Actually, I take that comment back. Can I do that? Can I take it back?"

There it was, that effortless charm.

He couldn't let himself be charmed. This was business. She was his employee – a very good, very important employee. "Of course. I never heard it, but if I had, I wouldn't have been offended." He looked down at himself. "My mom actually saw me on a video call the other day and asked if I'd forgotten what the sun looked like. I guess I'm not looking too good these days."

Rose peeked out from behind her menu. "Aw, she's worried about you working too hard. Are you close with your mom?"

He glanced up at her, then back at his menu. "I try to call at least twice a week."

"Ah."

He looked up. "What?"

"Nothing."

"Go on." He set his menu down. "Do you have another comment to make that you'll need to redact?"

She shrugged. "I just find it interesting that you deflected the question."

"What do you mean? I answered your question."

She pursed her lips and stared at him, as if weighing whether he could handle what she was going to say.

Apparently, she decided he could. "Answering the question would've been a *yes* or a *no*, followed by an explanation. You just gave me a semi-related statement about the frequency of your phone calls."

Craig laughed. She wasn't wrong. "I'm sorry. I don't think I'm the best communicator."

"Seems like something you need to practice." She turned her menu toward him and pointed at a pizza called The CheeseNado. "I think we have to get this because the picture looks *incredible*."

Again, she wasn't wrong. The pizza was layered with mozzarella, hand-dipped ricotta, blistered tomatoes, and sopressata. "Whatever you like. My treat."

A smile spread across her face. "Outstanding."

The waitress dashed over and, after they placed their order, Craig had a moment where he thought they were going to fall into an awkward silence.

He tried to think of something to say, but Rose beat him to it. "My mom died when I was little. I never got to know her." She stopped. "Not that I didn't have a mom. Her sister, Claire, adopted us. Us being me and my two sisters. My mom owns a hotel on the island. It's actually kind of a crazy story."

Craig had been taking a sip of his water and started to choke. "I'm sorry, what?"

"It's a long story."

He cleared his throat, recovering. "Please. I'd love to hear it."

She smiled, and his entire focus got pulled into Rose's erratic storytelling. She'd start with one part of the story, then get distracted by telling him some small detail, then jump back into the main story, or something else entirely.

It was a wild ride, but he enjoyed every moment of it.

When their pizza arrived, Rose's face was twisted into a frown.

"What's wrong?" he asked. "Is this not what we ordered?"

"No, it is. I just realized I've been talking this entire time. I must be boring you to death."

"Not at all. Your family is much more interesting than mine."

She lifted a slice of pizza from the pan and placed it on his plate, then served a slice for herself. "Tell me about them. What was your life like growing up?"

Normally, Craig would say something like, "It was good," or "I had the perfect childhood." These were his standard phrases, and people were satisfied by them because they didn't want to know more. Oftentimes, it felt like people were waiting for him to stop talking so they could go back to talking about themselves.

It wasn't that way with Rose, and he suspected she wouldn't be satisfied with a simple answer. She would try to analyze him, and beyond that, her being so forthcoming made him feel like he needed to reciprocate.

"My mom and dad both worked at a software company." He took a bite of pizza. The cheese burned the roof of his mouth, but he didn't care. It was too good. He took another bite.

She raised her eyebrows. "Oh, fancy. Tech jobs run in the family."

"Not exactly. My mom was a secretary and my dad was a janitor." He paused, waiting for her to react or look disappointed, but she didn't say anything. "They were with the company from the beginning, and stayed on as the place became huge. The CEO loved both of them and offered to pay for me to go away to private school."

"No way! Like boarding school?"

He nodded. "Starting from age ten, I spent most of the year living in Massachusetts."

Her jaw dropped. "That's so far away! You must've missed your parents so much."

He had, but being the eldest child, he'd never wanted to show weakness. "It was a great education, and I got to know a lot of kids from important families. Eventually, it paid off. I got into Princeton."

She took a bite of her pizza crust and set the rest down. "That's impressive. Your parents must be so proud."

He nodded. "Yeah. They are."

Rose sat back, her smile fading. "That's so much pressure for a little kid though. Did you feel like your family's success was on your shoulders?"

Suddenly the pizza felt very dry. Craig took a sip of water. "I guess you could say that."

She nodded, watching him.

"I still do." He sighed, wiping his hands on a napkin. "I've never actually told anyone that."

"Does it feel like there is a little bit of weight off your shoulders now?"

He laughed. "Not really, but it's nice to say it out loud."

"Here. Have more pizza." She pushed another slice onto his plate. "And keep talking."

He really wanted to keep talking. The look in her eyes made him really believe she wanted to hear about this.

But no. He wasn't going to bore her with his life. She couldn't possibly want to know this stuff. She was being polite. It was time to change the subject.

"There's nothing else to say." He cleared his throat. "How do you like your office?"

Chapter Twelve

A ha, she'd gone too far. Rose needed to be careful with what she said. Craig was her boss, after all. Not her friend.

It was her fault. She was giddy about the review Seymour had given her, happy about her new job and her first paycheck. Still, just because Craig was approachable and close to her age, it didn't mean –

"Wait. How old are you?" Rose asked as she grabbed another slice of pizza.

Craig raised his eyebrows, a glint in his eye. "How old do I look?"

She sat back and crossed her arms. "Nineteen."

A laugh burst out of him. "Close. Thirty-three."

"Oh good. For a second, I was scared you might be younger than me. That's been freaking me out recently."

He tilted his head to the side. "Who freaked you out by being younger than you? Did you have a surgery done by a child prodigy or something?"

"As my employer," Rose said slowly, wagging a finger, "you're not allowed to ask those kinds of questions. But yes, I had my funny bone replaced. What do you think?"

He laughed again and shook his head. "Phenomenal work. Top notch funny-ness."

"Thank you." It was a lame joke, but she couldn't stop herself sometimes. "It was Seymour, actually. The client. He was only twenty-five. Practically a baby."

"That baby was thrilled with your matchmaking services. How'd you do it?"

He didn't have to ask her twice. Rose told him how she'd gone through the system's matches, spent time talking to him, and even though she'd made up her mind not to tell anyone what she'd done, she confessed to meeting up with Seymour to help fix his wardrobe.

"I'm not going to do that with every client," she rushed to add, "so don't yell at me. It just seemed like he needed the help, and he really appreciated it."

Craig's eyes were focused but soft. "I'd never yell at you. It's not really my style."

Huh. No yelling. That was something.

Rose released the tension that had built up in her shoulders. She'd gotten used to yelling, for the most part. Her old boss liked to yell. It was the only way he knew to get his point across.

Now she wondered if all that yelling had made her preemptively afraid with everything she did. Perhaps that was the point.

Craig went on. "I'm blown away by how dedicated you are. I don't want to scare you, but you've even caught the attention of our potential buyer, Brett."

Rose Woodley would've been spooked. But Rose Woodson, imaginary as she was, wasn't scared of anything.

"Really?" She forced herself to sit up straighter. "Do you need me to meet with him? Show off a little?"

Show off a little? Who was she even pretending to be? She needed to tone it down.

"No." He cleared his throat. "I'm going to protect you from him as long as possible. He's..." Craig shook his head. "Hard to like. I don't want to put too much pressure on you."

Rose let out a breath. As thrilled as she was that Seymour's match had gone well, she had no idea if she could do it again.

In fact, the more she thought about it, the more it seemed certain that she *couldn't* do it again.

"Seymour said you asked him questions he'd never thought about before," Craig said.

"It wasn't anything earth-shattering. I asked him why he hadn't found a partner, and with some pushing, he was able to tell me. He was pretty self-aware." She paused. "Well, except for how he saw himself. People are so hard on themselves."

Present company included – but she kept that to herself.

He wiped his hands on his napkin and shrugged. "Maybe you just knew the right questions to ask."

She couldn't help herself. Rose leaned in, a smile tugging at her lips. "If I looked you in the eye right now and asked why *you* haven't found a serious, successful relationship, what would you say?"

Craig sat back. "What makes you think I'm not in a serious, successful relationship?"

Shoot. She'd done it again.

Rose shut her eyes. "I'm sorry. I was making assumptions. You're probably happily married."

After a beat, Craig's stern expression broke into a smile. "No, I'm messing with you. I'm single."

Interesting. The handsome, wealthy tech guy was more into the theory of relationships than he was into actually having them. He probably didn't have time.

Then again, Rose didn't want to assume. "Why is that?" she asked.

He shrugged. "Just haven't met the right person."

"That's what Seymour said until I pushed him."

Craig blinked a few times, frowned, then let out a breath. "I feel like I'm in the hot chair."

"You're not! I'm just giving you an idea of how I work."

She sat back, trying to contain her smile. If only Lucy and Lillian could see her now. She was talking as if she knew what she was doing, not as though she was a total fraud.

Craig kept his head down, staring at the one lonely slice of pizza left on the pan. "My last two girlfriends both said I was closed off." He looked up, his eyes locking onto hers. "It's partially why I made the app. I figured people could use it to get all those questions out of the way. It's stupid, I know. It doesn't replace getting to know someone."

"It's not stupid!" Rose launched herself forward and her hand ended up on top of his. She quickly snatched it away when she realized what she'd done. "Sorry, bad reflex. I tend to touch people. I don't mean anything by it."

He smiled an easy smile. "No problem."

It was strange to hear a calm, in-control guy like Craig admit to any sort of self-consciousness. Rose had reacted to that – to seeing a bit of herself in him.

"I think it's a brilliant system," Rose finally managed to say. "If people answer the questions honestly, they have a great chance at finding a 'right' person. A match."

He nodded and sat back, crossing his arms over his chest.

Rose had never seen him in anything but a suit. Now he was in a T-shirt, his muscles exposed and distracting. She stared at him, her mind blanking out for a moment...

No. Stop.

She was not doing that. There were a lot of ways she could mess this job up, the most spectacular being if she developed feelings for her boss.

He wasn't just her boss; he was one of the guys who'd started the company. There could be no dumber way to ruin a perfect gig.

He spoke again, jarring her from her thoughts. "Why haven't *you* found The One, Doctor of Love?"

She cleared her throat and forced herself to look down at her plate. "I can't tell you."

"Is that off-limits?"

Rose looked back up at him. He had a half-smile on his face and a playful expression in his eyes.

Why did she have to go and find such a cute boss?

She shook her head. "Nothing is off limits. I'm not even an open book – I'm a megaphone." She paused. "It's just...it'll make you think less of me."

He scrunched his eyebrows. "I doubt that, but I won't put you in the hot seat. I'm nicer than that."

"Okay, you've convinced me." She put her hands up. "I'm sort of stuck in a holding pattern with my ex-boyfriend. We broke up, but there's still a lot between us. You know how these things go."

"Oh." He was quiet for a moment, eyes wide. "I wasn't expecting that."

She tilted her head. "Why not?"

He grimaced and tapped his finger on the table. "It seems like..." Craig shrugged. "Like something you wouldn't put up with. The uncertainty, I mean."

"I'm not *putting up with it*," she said, using her fingers for air quotes. "Our timing has just been off. We're a great couple. Meant to be, really."

Rose stopped. She knew how this sounded. She should've stopped talking before she even started. Lucy and Lillian wouldn't have let her babble this long. "But there's your answer. That and the fact that I was bitten by a werewolf a few years ago and every month I run into the woods to hide my beastly form."

He grinned. "There's that funny bone acting up again."

"Guilty."

Craig motioned to the pan between them. "Do you want the last slice?"

Of course she did, but she didn't want to admit it. "No. You take it."

He studied her for a moment, then put it onto her plate. "I insist."

Was it better to eat the pizza, or to keep talking and making it sound like she was pathetically waiting for her ex?

Waiting for a guy didn't seem like something Dr. Rose Woodson would do...but she couldn't even show up for a TV interview on time. What did she know?

"I'm not going to fight you on it." She picked up the slice. "I can only assume this is the standard treatment for your star employee."

He nodded. "That's right."

Rose laughed. She wasn't sure who she was yet – star employee, pathetic ex-girlfriend, werewolf – but it didn't matter. All that mattered was staying focused and moving forward.

And that meant *not* finding Craig charming, or handsome, or fun...even if he was.

Especially if he was.

She took a bite of pizza. "Thanks, boss."

Chapter Thirteen

They'd had no business staying at the pizza place as long as they did, but Craig had completely lost track of time. He only realized it was late when he felt something bump into his shoe, looked down, and saw a broom.

"I'm so sorry, I didn't know it was closing time," he said, shooting out of his chair. "We'll get out of your hair."

The employee took it in stride. "I'm not kicking you out. Yet." She moved his chair aside and swept some crumbs. "You've got fifteen minutes. After that, I will *not* be shy about making you go, and I don't care if you leave a bad review."

She let out a gruff laugh, and Craig smiled. He had been in her position many times, though he never handled it as gracefully.

He'd just been a kid, after all. An anxious, insecure kid, the only one of his classmates at the boarding school who'd had to keep a job.

Whenever people wouldn't leave his old restaurant at the end of the night, he suffered in silence, tormented by their cluelessness. He was always in a rush to get back to the dormitories before anyone noticed he was gone, to shower before anyone noticed he reeked of onions and grease.

It was all part of his shame, and at first, when he went to Princeton, he hung out with a few classmates from his high school and tried to keep up the façade.

It wasn't until he'd met Barney that his perspective changed. He made new friends, and he didn't have to hide he was a janitor's son. No one cared.

Though Barney came from money, he wasn't spoiled. He introduced Craig to people from all over the country, all over the *world*, from different backgrounds and cultures. For the first time in his life, Craig could be himself.

Or at least, try to be himself. He was still a work in progress.

They walked outside into the cool evening breeze, a black sky hanging above them, the gravel of the parking lot crunching beneath their footsteps.

Craig walked behind Rose and spoke when they got to her car. "I'm sorry I took up your entire evening."

She made a face. "You're always apologizing. Don't be sorry. This was fun."

He scratched the back of his neck. "We hardly had time to talk about your plans for the next clients."

"That's true." Rose tapped her chin, then said, "I'm free tomorrow! We can meet up somewhere. I'll bring my computer and my notebooks. Maybe you can show me your parents' new house!"

Craig hadn't shown *anyone* the house yet, not even his own sister, but without thinking, he said, "Sure. That sounds good. I'll send you the address."

~

The next morning, Craig peeked through the front window, waiting for Rose to arrive. He'd had trouble sleeping, replaying the things he'd said, worrying about how she might've taken some of his comments.

Maybe he shouldn't have told her so much about his life? She could be silently categorizing him, psychoanalyzing his words, seeing through the excuses he'd made about his life.

It felt like Rose was the most dangerous employee at the company. She was too *smart.* It felt like she could see straight through him.

Beyond that, everyone was fascinated with her. People were clamoring to sign up for the service. Reporters were trying to sneak in. Even Brett felt entitled to her time.

And Craig... he wasn't immune to her charms, either. It was unfair, really. He'd spent a lot of time with her, and he was only human. It was so many little things – the way her eyes lit up right before she asked a question, the way she tilted her head back when she laughed, like she was really bursting with joy. How could he help but fall in love, just a tiny bit?

Maybe it was best to let her work alone. Slow things down. Put distance between them.

Craig was great at creating distance. He'd kept people away his entire life. He considered canceling, telling her he had been called off-island for business. His thoughts had reached a crescendo as he pulled out his phone, about to call Rose, when she appeared and honked her horn.

He had no choice but to open the door.

"This is amazing!" she yelled as she walked up the driveway. "The views are incredible, and the house is *so* pretty! I love what you've done with the siding."

"Thanks," he said, wringing his hands together. "They're cedar shingles. I think my parents will like them. I still want to do something with the landscaping. The weeds are really taking over this part of the yard."

She waved a hand. "That's nothing. I could dig those up for you in an hour. Did I tell you I worked on a landscaping crew for a year in college?"

"No." He tilted his head. "Were you a gardener?"

"I did gardening, weeding, mulching, and even built fences." She puffed out her cheeks. "If I never dig a hole for another fence post again, I will die happy."

Craig laughed. At least he wasn't the only one who'd suffered a crappy job. "Come on in. The internet is up and running, and I have folding chairs in the living room that will make your legs go numb after ten minutes."

"Lovely!"

He gave her a brief tour, slightly mortified by his rolled up sleeping bag in the bedroom, and she gave him recommendations for furnishing the place.

"It's not always the easiest to get furniture to the island," she said. "But I know some people." She paused and rolled her eyes. "Well, my mom knows some people, but it's the same thing, right?"

He laughed. "Yeah. Same thing."

He offered her the chair with a better view from the window, but Rose didn't take it. Instead, she opened her laptop on the floor, then proceeded to spread papers all around. "These are the potential clients I was thinking of working with next. Each one is color-coded with their responses, their needs, and their potential matches."

Craig stared, amazed she was able to find so many colors of Post-it notes.

"With Seymour, it took me a week to find his match," Rose said with a frown, "but I plan on speeding the process up."

He nodded. "Okay."

She kept talking, almost as if to herself. "On the other hand, not all the matches will happen as quickly as Seymour's, and there's always a chance that a match could break up. It's six months they have access to matchmaking, right?"

Craig nodded. "That's right." He suspected, however, that Rose knew the program better than he did.

"Ideally, once I'm up to speed, I'll be able to handle at least five active matches at once. My goal is to start two new matches each week, meaning I'll do about a hundred matches a year, give or take. I'm not sure if that was the number you were look-ing for, or if you'd like to see more?"

Craig sat back and sucked in a breath. "To tell you the truth, I was planning to see how it went. A hundred is more than I expected." He paused. "Though, right now, we have about three hundred people waiting to be selected for the service, and every one said they're willing to pay $10,000."

Rose's mouth popped open, and she quickly covered it with her hand. "I'm sorry. I must've blacked out, because I thought you said ten thousand dollars?"

"Oh, I thought I'd told you that. Sorry." Craig shrugged. "We're still in beta, of course, but to be able to meet demand, I think we'd have to increase the price to twenty or thirty thousand..."

Rose plopped into her chair with a thunk. "That's a million dollars. A *million* over a year...if you don't increase the price."

"We've only done one match, so we don't need to rush to quantify everything. It's fine to stay exclusive. We could have you train other matchmakers too, to lighten your load." He looked away from the window and saw that Rose was staring blankly ahead. He rushed to clarify. "If you want to. Whatever you prefer."

Rose cleared her throat. "No. Training other people could be good. Whatever you think is best for the company."

A weight sunk into his stomach. She must think he was angling to replace her. That wasn't what he'd meant at all.

He tried to come up with a better explanation, but Rose had already moved on, discussing the details on the next five clients she'd chosen. She had their preliminary matches and wanted to schedule her first meetings with each of them.

"Are there any changes you'd like me to make?" she asked, her eyes wide and bright. "I really take no offense if you want something done differently. I'd much rather know that I'm doing something wrong early on so I can fix it."

Try as he might, Craig had no advice to give her. She was the dream employee: organized, driven, and intelligent. When they were just starting, they always talked about hiring quality people, and it felt like he'd hit the jackpot.

How did he express to her how important she was, how pleased he was with her planning and execution?

He gave her a generic, "I think you're doing great."

She nodded, turning back to her computer screen. "Now that things are picking up, I can send you a summary at the end of each week with what I've been up to, if you'd like?"

"Oh. That'd be nice, not just for me, but for the board. I don't know why I didn't think of that."

He stopped. It felt like he was caught swimming with seaweed tangled in his legs. Why couldn't he get out what he wanted to say? She was a star, but every time he tried to assure her that she was far exceeding expectations, he fell flat.

He was afraid of saying *too* much. Afraid of giving away how he really felt about her, and her kind eyes and her laugh and her self-deprecation...

With these thoughts whirling in his mind, he started to speak, and something terrible happened.

Was it the warm glow of her conversation? The pleasing neatness of her color-coded stacks of papers? The way the light hit her hair?

Whatever it was, it didn't matter, because the words that came out of his mouth were, "How did it take me so long to find you?"

Chapter Fourteen

T he blush started in Rose's chest, spread to her neck, and finally reached her cheeks.

"I don't know, but I can't tell you how nice that is to hear." She took a deep breath, trying not to smile like a fool. She thought the blush had started deeper than in her chest – that perhaps it came from her soul.

Embarrassing.

"They never said nice things at my last job," she added. "I'm realizing my boss was kind of a monster."

Craig cocked his head to the side. "I thought you were teaching classes at Washington State?"

Shoot. Rose wasn't used to keeping track of a fake story. She was not a good liar. She talked so much it was impossible to keep track of untruths. "Yeah, you know. University politics."

"Or was that the landscaping place?"

Craig laughed, and Rose laughed too, eager to change the subject. "I've got a lot to do, so I'd better get back to work. Let me know when your parents arrive. Maybe we can put something together for them at the hotel. A warm welcome."

"I'm almost afraid of telling them about this house," he said. "They've always said it's their dream to live on the island, but I don't know how they're going to deal with the change.

Last week, my mom's whole day was ruined because she had to go to a new grocery store."

Rose could relate. All those years, staying at her miserable job, she'd convinced herself that it was better than the unknown.

She had been wrong, though. This was better. Whatever it was, wherever this wild ride took her, it was better.

"They will be thrilled. Even if it takes a while for them to realize it."

Rose excused herself and escaped to her car. There was too much to think about, too much overflowing from her mind.

Craig's words circled her thoughts. He was too sweet. The other employees loved him and she could see why. He was intelligent, trusting, and kind.

That was what her last boss had lacked. Kindness. He was driven, he was brilliant, but man, he was a jerk.

Still, Rose was certain Craig hadn't told her that the clients were paying *ten thousand dollars each*! If she succeeded in matching a hundred people a year – and that was a big *if* – she alone would bring a *million* dollars to the company.

It was enough to send her into a panic. It was a lot of pressure for someone who was a big, fat, fake.

And yet.

The first match had gone well, and Craig was impressed by what she had planned for the next clients.

That was what she had to focus on. Not the money, not the fact that she was a liar who talked too much and would surely out herself.

The work. She had to focus on the *work*, not Craig's kind eyes and his strong-looking arms, and wondering if he worked out, and of course he worked out, and wondering what it would be like to have those arms wrapped around her and to lay her head on his chest...

She shook her head, as if trying to shake out the thought. Being a romantic was all good and dandy when it helped her make matches for *other* people. It was not useful when she was trying to be a fake professional while having a cute boss.

No more of that, though. No more daydreams. She had to at least try to be serious and keep up the ruse of being professional, and she was getting close to finally reuniting with Greg. Nothing could mess that up.

~

Rose drove back to the apartment and was promptly dragged to a movie with Lillian and Lucy. It was nice to get her mind off things, and when she logged onto her computer bright and early on Monday morning, she felt ready for the million-dollar task ahead of her.

Her next client was a thirty-five-year-old woman named Jill Breyer. She'd started a company that produced children's songs and stories and had been a millionaire since her thirtieth birthday.

This information was all available in her public profile, along with pictures of her sipping cocktails in Crete, skiing in France, and hiking in Japan.

What hit Rose in the gut was the last line of her matchmaking application. "I don't have any kids of my own, despite desperately wanting them," she wrote, "and it feels like time is running out. Please help me!!"

Rose sent her a message and within a day, Jill wrote back, saying how delighted she was to be selected for the matchmaking service. She suggested lunch at an Italian eatery in Seattle the next day, and Rose didn't dare say no. She flew in and spent some time at the office, making sure to leave with time to spare.

Despite getting there ten minutes early, Jill had her beat. She stood and waved as soon as Rose walked into the restaurant.

Jill looked exactly like her pictures. She was tall, close to six feet, with sun-kissed skin and cascading locks of dark hair.

"It's so nice to meet you, Jill." Rose took her hand and got a firm handshake.

"You too. Rose, right? I'm going to call you Rose." She said, taking a seat. "I'm going to be honest, I don't have a lot of time for this, but I've tried everything. My last relationship was with a man twenty years my senior. I thought dating someone older meant he'd have life figured out, but eight months in, I discovered he'd been hiding something."

"Uh oh," Rose said, taking her seat. "Nothing big, I hope?"

"Oh, no." Jill nodded. "Just his wife and three children. No big deal."

"The nerve." Rose shook her head. "How did he manage to hide it so well?"

"He lived in New York and we didn't see each other very often." She waved a hand. "I thought it was the perfect relationship at the time because he wasn't needy. I find that all these guys are too *needy*. That or we go on one date and I never hear from them again."

Rose nodded. "Interesting. So you see a pattern?"

"Yes!" Despite not claiming to have time, Jill then went on for forty minutes, detailing her dating life and the failures until this point, even going as far as reading messages aloud from various rejected beaus.

When she got to present day, she let out a sigh. "I want to have kids, and I don't have time to mess around. I've already built my business, and now I need to build my family. Can you help me or not?"

A smile spread across Rose's face.

"What?" Jill sat back. "Is something about my situation funny to you?"

Rose shook her head and leaned forward. "No, not at all. I just that you remind me of my sister Lucy."

Jill took a sip of her lemon water, then slowly set the glass down. "Is that a good thing?"

"Lucy would say it is." Rose made sure to stop smiling. "She's also quite scary."

Jill's eyes narrowed and, for a moment, she was still.

Rose felt her insides run cold. Had she made the wrong move? Been too friendly? Too familiar?

But a moment later, Jill burst into a laugh, her first of the entire meeting. "You think I'm scary?"

Rose let out a breath. She was delighted, just like she hoped she'd be. "Yes. Even in your messages to some of these guys, you have a side of aggression."

"I'm not aggressive. I'm *direct*."

"When they don't know you, it's aggressive, especially coming from someone as successful and beautiful as you are," Rose said firmly.

Jill seemed to think on this, and she smiled. "Okay, Rose. Don't flatter me."

"I'm not flattering you. Not really. I'm trying to understand you. Who you are, what you need, why you need me."

She nodded. "Can you find me a match, then?"

"I can, but you have to trust me."

"Fine."

"And you have to be nice to him. Your match."

She groaned. "My sister is always saying that to me. But I am nice! What else am I supposed to do, roll out a red carpet for these guys?"

Rose laughed. "I just mean, just give the guy a chance. A real one. Go on a few dates, and don't interrogate him."

"Nice is overrated," Jill grumbled.

"You're an extremely impressive person," Rose said, pulling up Jill's SerenadeMe profile and scrolling through the pictures. "I'm going to match you with someone who is not impressed by you. At all."

Jill laughed. "Okay."

"You're probably not going to like him at first."

"Because you're going to match me with a loser?"

"There, right there," Rose said, pointing. "That's not nice."

She crossed her arms. "Fine. Why won't I like him?"

"Because I'm going to pick someone who will challenge you, and not in a business way. I'm guessing you're not used to that."

She uncrossed her arms, a bemused smile on her face. "Okay, matchmaker. Do your thing."

Chapter Fifteen

As much as she would've preferred staying in the cozy comfort of her bed, Lillian had to get up early that Sunday morning and get dressed for an aerial silks class.

It was all Lucy's doing. She'd gotten a deal on tickets and insisted on dragging both Rose and Lillian down – or was it up? – with her.

"We're allowed to just watch, right?" Rose asked, taking a bite of toast.

Lucy dumped a cup of frozen strawberries into the blender and answered without looking up. "No."

"Nice try," Lillian said under her breath. "We're going to be spinning around like spiders in a web."

"More like trapped flies," Rose whispered.

They both laughed and were soon drowned out by the blender going off. A minute later, Lucy slid each of them a glass of her famous strawberry protein shake.

"Drink up. You're going to need this to help your weak arms."

Rose's mouth popped open. "I don't have weak arms. They're strong enough to carry the weight of my sparkling personality, and also four frappuccinos from Starbucks at *once.*"

"Yeah! And I can open almost any jar in the house," Lillian added.

Lucy wasn't having any of it. She downed her drink, squinted briefly at the brain freeze, then picked up her keys. "Drink! We need to go. You are both going to have *fun* whether you like it or not."

Rose and Lillian exchanged glances before finishing their smoothies. It was going to be a long morning.

Lucy herded them into her car and drove them to the gym. The entire time, she talked about the instructor for the class – how she was only visiting for a few weeks before going back to the mainland, how gifted she was, and how very lucky they all were to get into such an exclusive event.

Lillian was more interested in how Rose was doing at her new job. It seemed like she was completely engrossed in her role and rarely even had time to answer texts until the end of the day.

At one point, while raving about the flexibility and strength they'd build on the silks, Lucy developed a cough and had to take a drink of water.

Lillian jumped at the chance to change the subject. "How was work this week, Rose?"

"Good!" Rose said, a smile spreading across her face. "I set up a date for my scary Lucy client."

"She sounds so cool," Lucy said wistfully. "Maybe she'd agree to be my mentor and then I could be a millionaire, too."

"No," Rose said firmly. "You don't want to be a millionaire."

"Says who?" Lucy shot a glance over her shoulder, eyes narrowed. "I'd be a great millionaire."

"You'd make us go to a lot more of these classes," Lillian said with a yawn. "I don't think I can get behind it."

Lucy laughed as she parked the car. "Yeah. I would."

They got out of the car and walked into the gym. There were four colorful silks hanging from the twenty-foot ceiling, with a lithe instructor already woven into and spinning around on one ten feet above the ground.

"Welcome," she called out, striking a pose with her leg sticking out. "Please pick a silk. Two of you will have to share."

"We'll share," Rose called out, then dropped her voice. "It'll be less work, hopefully."

"And I can catch you when you fall off," Lillian muttered.

Lucy chose a silk at the front of the class and immediately dropped onto the floor to stretch.

"Should we stretch, too?" Lillian asked.

Rose shrugged. "Can't hurt?"

They sat, legs extended, on the spongy floor and half-heartedly reached for their toes.

"I can't believe you told your new client she was scary," Lillian said. "Who *are* you?"

Rose leaned in, grinning. "I know! It's so unlike me. I don't know what's happening." She sighed, then sat back and looked at the ceiling. "It might be the fake PhD. It makes me feel invincible."

"I think your old job was holding you back."

"That could be it." She looked back down and clasped her hands in front of her. "Craig is an *amazing* boss. Everyone loves him and the other employees are so happy. It's so relaxed. I feel like he's always encouraging me, and he thinks everything I do is great."

It almost sounded like he liked her. A *lot*. It was so like Rose to be blind to it, too. Lillian was going to comment on this, but the instructor clapped her hands and shouted, "Everyone, let's get started. I'm going to guide you on a journey through the silks today."

Without realizing it, Lillian let out a groan.

Lucy turned around and glared at her.

"Sorry," she whispered.

The instructor grabbed at the long hanging silk in front of her with one hand. "You are going to learn to twist your body into a work of art, and then unravel to the ground as gracefully as a caterpillar morphing into a butterfly. It will look effortless, but every muscle in your body will be screaming in pain."

"Just what I wanted to hear," Rose whispered, and Lillian snorted a laugh.

Lucy shot her another look, but quickly returned her focus to the front of the class. It was time to begin.

"Reach up and climb," the instructor said in a sing-song voice as she vaulted up the silk like a bug on a wall. "Get to know your silk!"

"You first," Rose said.

"No, you!" Lillian pushed the fabric toward her and it swung wildly between them.

"*Fine*," Rose said, "but only because I'm Rose Woodson, PhD, climber of the silks."

She took a deep breath, rubbed her hands together, and jumped as high as she could. For a moment, she had a hold of the silk, but within seconds, she came crashing to the ground.

Lillian covered her mouth with her hand, trying not to laugh.

"It's okay," the instructor said, appearing at their side. "Try again."

Rose nodded. "Sure. Yeah, okay. One more time."

"This time, wrap the material around your foot and use that to climb up, inch by inch."

Rose fumbled with the silk, managing to get it around her foot after a ten-second struggle.

The instructor tugged it tight. "Now go!" she said. "Trust the silk to raise you higher."

Miraculously, Rose went up, inching like a worm. "Hey, I'm doing it!"

Lucy waved from her silk, five feet off the ground. "Nice work!"

The instructor returned to the front of the class, leaping into position. "Now we are going to turn our worlds upside down and get a new perspective!"

"Oh no, we aren't," Rose grumbled, and both she and Lillian had to look away so as to not break into a fit of giggles.

Four minutes later, Rose returned to the ground with shaking arms and cheeks reddened from exertion. "Don't be fooled by my grace," she said. "That's the hardest thing I've ever done."

Lillian looked up. "I'm not doing it."

"You have to. Lucy will end you."

"Maybe Mom needs us? I'll go check my phone."

"Allow me." Rose held up a hand. "I need some water."

Rose scampered off, returning a moment later with her phone in her hand. "I have to go."

"No, you are *not* leaving me here."

"It's for work! Look!" She held up her phone. "Someone had a terrible date with SerenadeMe and posted a video about it. It's gotten four *million* views! This is going to kill our stock prices."

"Listen to yourself!" Lucy appeared behind them. "*Our* stock prices. Like you own the company."

"I feel responsible," Rose said. "I care, you know."

Lucy snorted. "I can't tell if you're serious."

"I can't either." Rose tapped her chin. "Wait, yeah. I care. I really do, and I have an idea."

"Was it one of your clients?" Lillian asked. That would be bad. It could really throw Rose off, and she was just getting started.

"Thankfully, no. But I think I can fix it." She jogged off, gathering her things. "Sorry," she said, "but duty calls!"

"Wait!" Lillian yelled. "Take me with you!"

It was too late. Rose disappeared through the door as she yelled, "I'll be back in a few minutes!"

Lucy placed a hand on Lillian's shoulder. "Get up there. I'll spot you."

Lillian sighed, looking up. It was really happening.

"Get your foot in there," Lucy insisted, looping the silk around Lillian's foot.

"All right." She'd have to wait to hear about the excitement later. There were silks to wrestle. "I'm going, I'm going."

Chapter Sixteen

T he gym was stifling and hot – too much sweat from too many bodies crowded together.

Rose hated gyms. She took a seat outside on a bench and breathed in the cool air before searching online for the video from the news story. It took her a minute to find it, but the mortifying title was quite specific. "SerenadeMe matched me with a CREEP!"

Rose cringed. Creeps were bound to pop up, but it didn't make it any less painful. She clicked play and watched the forty second video, cringing the entire time. Then she watched it again.

The date was bad from start to finish. The guy showed up looking nothing like his pictures, so much so that the woman suspected he'd stolen them from a friend. Then he offered her a drink he'd "brought from home to save money," took offense when she wouldn't try it, and told her to stop being paranoid because it would be easy for him to track her car and figure out where she lived anyway.

For a date that lasted all of thirty minutes (the time it took the woman to pay her tab and sneak off to her car), it truly was awful.

Rose sat for a while, scrolling through the comments on the video and wondering what SerenadeMe could possibly do to prevent something like that from happening again. Panic buttons in the app? Facial recognition software for new users? Creep reports?

She vaguely remembered hearing about safety initiatives during her first week, but she couldn't remember much of it. She had an idea, and it was building like a wave.

Surely Craig wouldn't mind a quick call to brainstorm?

She dialed, figuring even if he answered, he was probably busy and –

"Rose. Hey!"

Not so busy, it seemed. "Hey Craig. Did you see the SerenadeMe creep story?"

He sighed. "Yeah. I heard about it yesterday. We've got security looking into this guy's account. We're not sure who he is yet – it looks like he used a stolen email. We're not sure what his deal is."

"Ah. Do you work with other apps to ban known nuisances?"

"You'd win the Nobel Peace Prize if you could get companies to get along like that," he said with a laugh. "The board's nervous about what's going to happen when markets open on Monday, but I don't think it's that big of a deal. Bad dates happen."

Though she technically agreed with him about the inevitability of bad dates, she had to disagree. "But it *is* a big deal! Our app matched her with a weirdo! Told her he was her soulmate! Can you imagine how demoralizing that must be?"

"Er..." He let out a small laugh. "I guess I didn't think of it that way."

"I have a plan. Let me find her a match. We can waive the fee."

"I don't think that's a good idea," he said. "But I appreciate you trying."

"Why not? Is it the money?"

"No, I don't care about that. I just – I think it'll blow over on its own."

Rose sighed. "Don't you think this could be an opportunity? If we get it right, it's free publicity."

What Rose should have said was, "If *I* get it right," but she couldn't bring herself to think that way. It would freak her out and make her freeze up. It felt better to be part of something.

He was quiet for a moment. "It could be bad publicity if we make her angrier. What if you talk to her and all she wants to do is berate you so she can post a video of that online, too?"

Rose frowned. "Why would she do that?"

"To get attention. We don't know if her story is true. She could have a website that she wants to promote or a shop selling knitted hats...I don't know. She might be using this whole thing as a way to launch her own brand."

Hm. All things Rose hadn't thought of in her excitement. What were the chances, though, that this woman was a fraud? Rose was the fraud in this scenario. There could only be room for one.

Hopefully.

The sun was starting to peek out from behind the clouds. She slipped on her sunglasses and stared at the too-blue sky.

"What I'm saying," Craig added gently, "is that I don't think it's worth your time."

She wasn't sure if Craig was savvier than her or if he just had a more suspicious mind. Maybe both.

Regardless, he was her boss. He ran the show.

"Okay," she finally said. "It was worth a shot."

They ended the call and she sat admiring her view for a minute before pulling up the video again. Even if Craig was right, it felt wrong to not reach out at *all* after one of their clients had such a bad experience.

The woman's first name was Annalise, and from the background of her video, it looked like she was in Chicago.

How many Annalises could there be on the app? Rose could probably find her if she could get to her computer. She wouldn't talk to her or anything – she wouldn't go against Craig's instructions – but maybe she could look at her answers for matchmaking. See what she was looking for. See if there was a non-creepy match for her out there, just waiting...

The door to the gym opened and Lillian popped her head out. "Lucy wants you to watch her twirl to the ground."

It would have to wait.

Rose stood. "Coming!"

~

It took Rose twenty minutes to find Annalise's profile on Monday, and another two hours to weed through the potential match list and narrow it down to twenty.

Rose found the guy Annalise had been matched with, too. Though his profile didn't have any red flags, she was able to find a lot of warnings about him in a Chicago Facebook "Are We Dating the Same Guy?" group. Apparently, he'd been creeping women out for the last two years using various apps.

When Craig dropped by her office after lunch, Rose rushed to hide her screen and cover the papers on her desk.

"What's going on? Everything okay? Do you need me?" she asked all at once, the guilt plain on her face.

Craig didn't seem to notice. He took a seat and shook his head. "You were right. The video *is* a big deal. Six million views now, and our stock price just took a hit. Brett is trying to use it as leverage to drop his price."

"Oh no!" Rose paused. Should she or shouldn't she tell him what she'd been up to?

What would Dr. Rose Woodson do?

"I might have good news for you," Rose said, slowly pulling a stack of papers out from under a book. "I took a look at Annalise's profile, and I think I can find her a good match."

He raised his eyebrows. "Oh?"

"I didn't do anything yet. I just wanted to see if she was a fake, and I don't think she is." Rose rushed to explain what she'd found out about the woman, the man, and the bad date they'd had.

She handed him a stack of papers with her research. "Let me offer the matchmaking service to her. If she's still mad, then so be it. She can yell at me a little. I can handle that."

For a minute – a long minute – Craig was quiet, leafing through the papers Rose had printed and marked, a frown fixed on his face. Finally, he looked up at her and locked eyes. His beautiful, intense hazel eyes.

Her heart jumped.

"We're going to need the PR team to be in the room," he said, rubbing his chin. "And legal. They'll have to listen in on the call and make sure you don't say anything that can get us into trouble."

Whoa. Rose didn't want people listening to their conversation. How awkward. How *weird*!

Worst of all, what if one of those people realized what a con she was?

Rose opened her mouth to speak, but her tongue was dry and stuck to the roof of her mouth. She took a sip of water and watched as Craig flipped through the pages again.

"The longer we sit on this, the worse it looks," he said, standing and tossing the papers onto her desk. "You were right, and I'm really glad you have all of this ready. Maybe we can do the call today? See if she's available. I'd love to see you at work."

He smiled and Rose forced herself to smile back. "Yeah, of course! I'd love that, too." Then she heard herself say, "Let's do it!"

Chapter Seventeen

E ven the customer service department was afraid to contact Annalise. The most they would do was send her an email offering for Rose to call her.

Luckily, she accepted and agreed to chat that afternoon. Craig was on his way to Rose's office when the lead from the security team caught up with him.

"Hey, we've been working with the programmers to add the user verification we talked about. It should go live in a few days and prevent another situation like this."

"Excellent work," Craig said. "I think it'll help with weeding out fake profiles. I really appreciate how quickly you guys worked on this."

"No problem! It's been kind of exciting. Uh, not that I *like* company disasters, but...you know."

Craig laughed. "Yeah, I know what you mean."

He got to Rose's office and slipped inside. Two staff members – one from legal and one from public relations – were already talking to Rose.

"We want to make sure you don't admit fault," the lawyer said.

She was a newer hire, and Craig hadn't worked much with her yet, but she looked the part: a black suit, a neat ponytail, and an unsmiling face. "You need to stress that reaching out to her is a courtesy. She needs to know that."

The PR manager cut in. "At the same time, you have to let her know we care. Everyone at SerenadeMe is on her side."

Rose's eyes were fixed on the notepad in front of her, her hand whipping back and forth as she scrawled notes. She paused, underlining something three times.

Craig took a few steps closer to see what it was. **It's not our fault, but we're on your side.**

Not the easiest message to get across.

She paused and looked up, spotting him, the tension on her face breaking into a small smile. "Hey, boss. Anything to add?"

"No," he said, leaning back against a bookshelf. "Are you ready for this? I can jump in if you like."

He had no idea why he'd offered that, because if there was anyone who could mess up a delicate conversation, it was him. But there it was.

Thankfully, she said, "No. I think I'm good."

"Okay!" The lawyer clapped her hands. "The clock just struck three. We'll be quiet in the background, but if you need us, just mute the call and put her on hold."

Rose made a face. "I'm not going to put her on hold."

"We might need to debrief," the PR manager said, nodding. "She'll understand."

Craig stuck out his tongue, but only Rose saw. She bit her lip and turned away, hiding a smile.

"I'll call her on speaker," she said, dialing out. She shuffled with her papers as the phone rang, loud and hollow, echoing in the room.

Was she nervous? Craig shifted his weight and tried to get a better look at her face. He didn't want to overwhelm her, but it seemed like she could handle anything. No one else was brave enough to face this woman.

A voice answered, flat and low. "Hello."

"Hi. Is this Annalise?"

A pause. "It is."

"This is Rose from SerenadeMe. Thanks so much for taking the time to talk to me today."

Her tone brightened. Slightly. "Sure."

The lawyer waved her hand and whispered, "Recorded line!"

Rose stirred, sitting up straighter. "I do have to let you know we are on a recorded line for quality purposes."

Craig winced. What a painful statement to have to interject. What else was legal going to make Rose say?

He had full faith in her, but he was feeling more uneasy about this conversation going well for anyone.

"Uh. Okay."

Rose took a deep breath. "Listen, Annalise. I watched your video and I felt awful. I wanted to do something to make it up to you."

The PR manager tapped a pen on her notepad, pointing at the phrase, "I'm here to improve your SerenadeMe experience."

Rose kept her head down, pretending not to see.

Smart.

"Well," Annalise said slowly, "Can you make sure that guy doesn't find out where I live and jump out of my closet while I sleep?"

Rose frowned. "If you need to place a restraining order, I can connect you with the Chicago PD. My specialty, however, is matchmaking."

"Yeah, I heard. I'm not interested. I've seen what you people do." She sighed. "I don't know what I expected from this call, but I don't need some overpriced call center operator trying to make me feel better."

Craig took a step forward. That was enough. There was no point in talking to this woman. She was hostile. Rose didn't deserve that.

He realized he was clenching his jaw and released it, raising a hand to get Rose's attention.

She didn't look up.

"I took a look at your profile," Rose continued. "You said you've watched all your friends find love. You're sick of being alone, sick of booking single seats on airplanes, sick of pretending like you don't like going to the movies because it's not as fun when you don't have someone to laugh with. Right? Those were your words?"

The PR manager's mouth was hanging open. Craig had to look away so he didn't laugh out loud.

Rose went on. "You said you're done waiting. You want to meet your husband and make your own happily ever after."

"I forgot I wrote that," Annalise said. "I must've been drinking."

"Give me one chance, *one* date. I'll match you with someone awesome. I can't promise he'll be your husband, but there's a chance he could be and your search will be over. I'll also do a background check and vet him myself so you don't get any surprises."

There was silence for a beat, then Annalise said, "Ah, I don't know."

Rose looked up, caught Craig's eye, and winked.

He grinned. She was about to close the deal. He didn't know how, but he could feel it.

Rose leaned into the phone. "What do you have to lose?"

Why was she so good at this? Was it because her old boss yelled at her so much? Was she just super skilled at defusing tense situations? Or maybe she was really a salesman and had him fooled.

Annalise was quiet. It seemed like the line had gone dead, but then her voice came through. "Fine. Why not. Let's do it."

Rose squealed. "Yay! You won't regret it."

It was clear Rose didn't need him to micromanage her every move. She was brilliant all on her own. Any excuse he made to watch her work was just that: an excuse.

He was playing a dangerous game. Maybe she didn't know why he was spending so much time with her, but he knew, and it had to stop. He was her boss and he was the COO of this company. He couldn't spend his time pining after her. It was a waste of time, and inappropriate.

Craig allowed himself to stare at her for one last moment before slipping out of the room.

~

Craig did an excellent job staying away from Rose and found many ways to fill his time. In the meantime, Rose got Annalise on a date ten days later, and within a month, her review was in.

The match went brilliantly. Rose had done it again, and Annalise released a video detailing how she met her Prince Charming through SerenadeMe's matchmaker. "Seriously, I had my doubts, but it was *amazing*. I take back everything I said. I guess you really do have to kiss a few frogs before you find your Prince Charming. Not literally, because ew, but you know."

By the end of the week, the video had more views than the original, and the matchmaker service had over five hundred new applicants.

Craig was reeling with the news when Barney walked into his office and dropped a newspaper onto his desk. The headline was **MYSTERIOUS MATCHMAKER ELEVATES DATING APP TO A MATCH-MADE-IN-HEAVEN.**

The author didn't know much about the "mysterious matchmaker," but they detailed how SerenadeMe's stock prices had increased twenty percent.

"You struck gold with Rose," Barney said. "She's incredible. We're on top of the world, man!"

Craig nodded. "I know. I can't believe it."

"I'm going to retire. In three months, I'm going to get on a boat and you'll never see me again. We just have to close this deal with Brett and we're out."

He could never discuss this with Barney, but Craig was starting to wonder if he was going to miss working at SerenadeMe. He liked the employees, even the pushy ones from PR and legal, and he enjoyed responding to problems and crises. What would he do with himself in retirement? Craig didn't want to own a boat. He could barely swim.

"But we've got a problem," Barney said.

Craig snapped out of his daydream. "What's that?"

"Brett's insisting on meeting Rose. Says she's a company asset."

That *was* a problem. "Tell him he can meet her when he buys the company. She's a company secret."

Barney laughed. "That's not going to work. He's been here almost every day this week, making up reasons for meetings. He says he needs to get to know every department."

Craig rubbed his face with his hand. As impressed as he was with Rose, and as good as she was with handling everything they threw at her, she didn't need to get dragged into this deal. She didn't need to jump through hoops for Brett or have his beady eyes watching everything she did.

"Can't do it," Craig said.

"We don't have a choice." Barney shrugged. "What's the big deal? Let him sit with her for a day or two. He says he wants a match of his own. Let him have the royal treatment, see how it all works."

He waved a hand. "Rose is too valuable."

A scowl formed on Barney's face, his stare fixed. "Craig."

"What?"

"You let Brett sit with the programmers for a day. And with PR."

"That was different. They loved it," Craig argued. "I could hear them laughing from down the hall. I think the programmers are convinced he's a real cowboy."

Barney tapped his hand on the desk. "This is something else. You're being weird."

"I'm not being weird. Rose...just...we can't risk losing her."

"I'm surprised you trust her so much."

Craig had to hold himself back to keep his temper from flaring. "What's that supposed to mean?"

Barney put his hands up. "Nothing. Why are you being so touchy?" He sighed. "I just mean – you don't trust anyone, usually. Except me. You have a problem with that."

"Well, maybe I'm expanding my boundaries?" Craig laughed. "Maybe I realized I needed to learn to count on other people."

"Ah." Barney nodded slowly. "Because you can't count on me anymore."

"No, it's not like that. I think it's just clear we've needed help for a while, and Rose has proven she's worthy of being trusted."

Barney was quiet, weighing this, before finally responding, "Yeah. You're right."

Crisis averted. Or so he hoped.

He was being too obvious with how he was treating Rose. He'd treated her differently from the beginning. But she *was* different...

"Can she at least talk to Brett? Smooth things over? He's not going to let this go."

Craig didn't like it. Not at all. The more he got to know Brett, the less he liked him. He dreaded meetings with him. The guy was just unpleasant. He didn't want Rose to have to deal with him.

But what could he do?

"Fine. I'll talk to her."

"Thank you." Barney cleared his throat. "Now do you want to go boating with me this weekend?"

"No, but thank you," Craig said with a laugh.

He had to find a way to break the bad news to Rose. He couldn't protect her forever. He realized that, logically.

At the same time, he had to wrestle with the urge to call off the deal entirely so Rose would never have to deal with Brett breathing down her neck.

If only.

Chapter Eighteen

Greg's email for their upcoming dinner was so business-like. Rose couldn't decide if he was trying to be funny, or if he was just being organized and unlike himself.

She was staring at her screen, lost in thought, when the door to her office burst open. Rose looked up with a start and saw Craig standing there, his skin pale and his eyes red.

A jolt ran through her.

They hadn't had much time to talk over the last few weeks. She was busy with matchmaking and Craig told her she had his full trust to deal with the clients. It was just the excuse she needed to keep herself from making excuses to see him.

But now, something had happened. Something *terrible*.

Had someone died? Worse – had her secret gotten out?

She didn't have a chance to play it cool. She stood from her seat. "What's wrong?"

Craig paced to the window, then abruptly spun and looked at her. "Nothing. Everything's going great. That's the problem."

A weight lifted from her chest. He hadn't found out her secret. Not yet.

"Oh." Rose cleared her throat. "Did you have a visit from a fortuneteller? Get some bad news?"

He took a seat across from her, his face sullen. "Not exactly."

"They're not so different from matchmakers, you know. Just trying to give people what they want." She paused and waited for him to smile, to say something clever back, but instead he wrung his hands together, let out a grunt and said, "That's true."

Not in the mood to joke. She sat back down. "What's up?"

He leaned forward, eyes downcast. "It seems like this deal is going to go through, and Brett is insisting on meeting with you. He read the story in the paper and says you're a company asset."

"Oh. Is that all?" Rose took a breath and released the tension from her shoulders. That was *nothing* compared to being found out to be a fraud and a con artist. "I don't mind. Unless you're afraid I'll mess it up."

He peered up at her, a smile finally cracking his stony expression. "How could you even think that?"

Her heart trembled, a useless flutter, like a butterfly against her ribs.

It was just nerves. She wasn't used to living a lie. "Why are you so afraid of me meeting him, then?"

"I don't know." He sighed, his head hanging low. "I'm not sure about this deal in general, and I have no one to blame but myself. I'm the one who lured Brett here in the first place. I'm the one who convinced him he wanted to buy the company."

"It can't be that bad. *He* can't be that bad." She paused. "Especially if we'll all be working for him soon."

Craig was quiet for a moment. "I think it's what it is. I don't like him, and I don't want to give him my baby."

Rose couldn't help herself. "I'm not a baby, Craig. I'm thirty years old."

This time he laughed, a real, hearty laugh. "I don't mean you, obviously. I mean the app. The company. All of SerenadeMe." He sighed. "I love this place. I know it's just a silly dating app, and in the grand scheme of things, none of it matters – but I love the people here. I care about them, and I love what we've built."

"Do you *have to* sell to Brett?"

"At this point, yeah. Brett seemed fine at first, but then...I got to know him." He leaned his head down again, rubbing his face with his hands. "Now it's not up to me. We're a publicly traded company, so we have to do what's in the best interest of the investors."

"And they want to sell to Brett?"

"Yes, the board wants to." He nodded. "Barney would sell to anyone at this point, he's so desperate to retire."

"Retire?" Rose laughed. "He's not even thirty-five years old."

"I know, but he put everything into building this company, and now he's got nothing left to give."

She winced. "That's bleak."

"It is." He sat, his shoulders slumped, his eyes downcast. "I'm the idiot who thought he could fix everything."

It looked like he needed a hug. Rose clenched her hands under her desk, trying to resist the urge to get up and wrap her arms around him. "You're not an idiot. Not at all."

He scoffed. "Thanks."

Do not hug your boss. You are not allowed to hug your boss. "So what if they want to sell to Brett? What do you want?"

He looked up at her, his eyes wide, his hair tousled. "It doesn't matter what I want." Craig stood and buttoned his suit jacket. "I'm sorry. I shouldn't have dumped this on you. I'm just...I needed you to know that I'm genuinely sorry you have to deal with Brett."

"I believe you," she said with a small smile. "You're forgiven."

His eyes met hers for the briefest of moments and that butterfly took off again.

Quiet, little butterfly.

"He's going to be here this afternoon," Craig said. "Can you meet with him?"

"Absolutely. I'll tell him I'm doing experiments on all the clients and scare him away. Problem solved."

A weak smile flickered on his face. "Ha. Yeah. That would be nice. Good luck, and again, I'm sorry."

He disappeared from her office and Rose stood, trying to stuff away the unsettled feeling in her chest.

There wasn't time to deal with things like *feelings*. There were reports to prepare. Figures to create. And, whether she liked it or not, a new boss to impress.

Maybe Brett wouldn't be all that bad. Maybe she'd feel the urge to give him a hug one day, too.

At least that's what she told herself as she got to work.

~

Brett showed up for their meeting ten minutes early and let himself into her office.

"Woo-eee!"

Rose startled. She couldn't believe she hadn't heard him coming. She also couldn't believe Craig didn't warn her about how he dressed.

He stood staring, both hands perched on his belt. "I finally get to meet the secret matchmaker."

He was not at all what she expected. Instead of showing up in a stuffy suit, he wore a light blue Western shirt with a navy yoke at the shoulders, a cowboy hat, and black boots with golden tips. The skin under his eyes was shiny and puffy, and while she'd assumed Brett was the name of a young, tech-startup-type man, he was closer to retirement age.

She momentarily forgot her manners, but finally said, "Please. Come on in."

"I will," he said with a wink, his voice deep and drawling.

He took a seat, and the reality of him buying the company hit her all at once. Instead of Craig sitting in the chair across from her, sighing and fretting, it would be this loud-talking cowboy.

Since she loved this job, she tried telling herself Brett might be more huggable than he looked at first glance.

He took off his hat. "I've been waiting ages for this meeting. Really. I'm wondering what it is you even do."

"I've only been here a few weeks," she said with a smile, "but I have a lot to show for it."

"I heard you got a million people banging on your door, begging to get a match."

"Not quite a million, but a lot, yes." She stood and handed him a folder of documents she'd prepared. "I've put together some information about my process and what we – "

"I'm not a numbers-and-charts kind of guy." He shook his head and dropped the folder onto her desk. "I'm more hands-on, if you know what I mean."

She didn't.

He leaned in, a wide, toothy grin opening his lips. "What I was hoping was for you to find me a match."

Oh. "A match?"

"That's right. I'm looking for my honey. Shouldn't be too hard, but you'll have to weed through the gold diggers." He chuckled.

There was something black between his front teeth.

"There's a lot to consider," she stammered.

He licked his lips. "How you feel about gold, Rose? Are you a rose gold kind of girl?"

She had no idea what he was talking about, and shamefully, in moments like these, a schoolgirl-like laugh tended to escape from her. "Ah, I don't know."

"What do you say?" he asked. "You think you can find a match for an old man, or are you not good enough?"

Okay, Rose understood why Craig didn't want to subject her – or *anyone* – to this man. He was baffling to talk to. It felt like as soon as she had a hold of the conversation, he abruptly changed course and walked off in the other direction.

It was exhausting, and the longer the conversation went, the more she wanted to escape.

She'd do whatever he wanted to make him go away. "Sure, yeah. We can make a match. I'll have you fill out the question-naire."

He shook his head. "No questionnaire, but you can ask me anything you want to know and I'll tell you."

Why did people think that was a generous offer?

She forced a smile, then turned to her computer and pulled up the questionnaire anyway. It would give her starting point, and something to return to when he derailed her thoughts.

Brett sighed and made a face. "Do we have to hang around this stuffy office? Aren't you hungry?"

She'd forgotten to eat lunch again, but she'd never admit to it. "Oh no, I'm fine. I can get through this quickly if you need to go."

"Let me take you to dinner. Everything is better over a bit of food, isn't it?"

She looked around, trying to think of an excuse. She had nothing. "No, I think—"

He stood and waved a hand. "Aw, come on. I know a place. You're going to love the lobster."

Rose hated lobster. "It's really okay," she said weakly.

"You're not gonna pull that with me. Come on. We gotta get some meat on you."

There was nothing Rose liked less than people commenting on her weight, but this comment at least made him seem a bit grandpa-ish.

She could humor a grandpa. "Let me get my purse."

Brett chattered the entire walk out of the office and didn't stop through the elevator ride or as they walked into the garage, where a fancy-looking SUV was waiting.

They sat in the back, and Rose wasted no time. She pulled out her laptop and started going through the questions.

"Since I don't have any of your demographic information, how old are you?"

"That's a funny question, young lady. How old are you?"

"Old enough to know better than to answer that," she said with a smile, mostly because she was unsure how old she'd have to be to pass as the actual Dr. Rose Woodson. "I'm going to put you down for...sixty."

He pondered this for a moment, then nodded. "Deal."

"Any previous marriages?" she asked.

"Next question."

He'd been bulldozing her from the moment he'd walked into the office. She needed to take control of the conversation. "There's no skipping questions."

"I said *next*!" He laughed and poured himself a drink from the side console.

"No answers, no match," she said firmly.

He took a swig of his drink. "All right, all right. I've been divorced, but just the one time."

"Any kids?" She asked, hoping he'd say something like, "I've got a daughter your age."

Instead, he said, "Not yet, but here's to hoping."

Rose typed that exact quote.

He was more compliant with the rest of the questions, though he tended to veer into long, rambling stories which Rose found difficult to rein in.

They got to the restaurant and she pressed on, desperate to look like a professional. By the time the appetizers arrived, she'd managed to get through all the questions.

"Those were the standard questions, but I also have my own." She paused. "Though I'm not sure I should share my trade secrets so easily."

He laughed, and a bit of bread shot out of his mouth and landed on the white tablecloth. "You're a smart one. I like that."

"Thank you." She cleared her throat. "I feel like I've learned a lot about you over the last..." She looked at her watch. "Two hours, but let me ask you this. What are you looking for in a relationship?"

He swallowed the bread and smacked his lips. "Smart, successful, young, and beautiful."

That was more of a shopping list, but okay. Rose kept her eyes focused on her computer screen. "Right."

"You don't have to be shy. I like a good, successful woman."

Uh... "I'm sure I can find you a good match."

"There's no need. I already know what I want. I'm looking right at her."

Rose kept her eyes straight as the walls closed in around her. This was *not* happening!

Before she could sputter out an answer, a miracle occurred. Craig appeared at the edge of their table. "Rose! We've been looking all over for you. We've got a matchmaking emergency."

"An emergency?" She looked up at him, wide-eyed.

Brett scoffed. "There can't be matchmaker emergencies."

Craig winked at her. "Sorry, bud. This is the business. You'll understand one day."

Rose followed his lead and stood from her seat.

"We were having a nice time," Brett protested. "You can't cut our dinner short. Rose is starving. Look at her."

Rose slipped her laptop into her purse. "I'm actually fine but thank you. I'll be in touch!"

She turned and walked out, shoulder to shoulder with Craig.

When they got through the front doors and onto the sidewalk, Rose burst into laughter. "You have *no* idea how you just saved me. Brett said he wanted me to find him a match, but it turned out he'd already decided *I* was his perfect match."

Craig groaned. "I am so, *so* sorry. I should've known this would happen with him."

"At first I thought he was sort of an eccentric grandpa," she said, "but *then...*" She shuddered. "I'm naïve, aren't I?"

"No." Craig laughed. "No one should have to anticipate that."

"Oh, you mean anticipate your future boss insisting on dating you? Yeah, no thanks."

The smile on his face faded and he cleared his throat. "I am sorry I cut off your dinner, though. Are you hungry?"

She pursed her lips, then turned to look at him. "I think you do owe me a pizza."

His smile returned. "You read my mind."

Chapter Nineteen

C raig didn't know what was worse – that Brett had hit on Rose or the fact that he hadn't prevented it.

Maybe the worst moment was when Rose talked about a boss dating an employee and her face twisted in disgust?

There was no need to choose. It was all bad, and Craig felt awful, even when Rose assured him she wasn't fazed.

"He caught me off guard," she said. "That was all, but I can handle him. Don't worry."

All Craig had were worries, but he wasn't going to burden her with them. Barney had been right about that – Craig wasn't in the habit of counting on others. It wasn't Rose's responsibility to fix this. It was his.

It was undeniable now, though. He couldn't let Brett buy the company. Even though it had been Craig's idea initially, he now knew it was a bad one. It didn't matter how desperate Barney was getting; with the fanfare around their matchmaker service, it should be easy to attract another buyer. Someone normal. The users deserved better. His employees deserved better.

Rose deserved better.

All he had to do was find someone. Barney would be happy, the company would be in good hands, and he could leave with a clear conscience.

Plus, he wouldn't be Rose's boss anymore and maybe she wouldn't find it so horrifying if he asked her out...

No.

That wasn't the reason to do it. He needed to fix his mistake, to deal with the rat he'd let in. It was the right thing to do, and no one else needed to be dragged into it.

~

Craig started on this project immediately and worked tirelessly into the night, then got up early and got into the office before anyone else arrived. He didn't let himself get distracted by anything – except for the one thing that was out of his control. The one place he couldn't keep his mind from wandering to: Rose.

No matter how many times he told himself to stop thinking about her, he couldn't do it. He'd be lost in thought, analyzing market caps, and find himself dreaming up excuses to see her, inventing reasons to be in the warm glow of her presence.

It was absurd. He had real problems, real people counting on him, and yet he had to fight himself from making trips to Starbucks just in case she might want something.

When the weekend arrived, he got a brief reprieve from his madness. It was finally time to show his parents their new house, and while he hoped it would be a joyous occasion, some worries still haunted him.

For instance, did his parents actually want to move to Orcas Island, or had it been a daydream? Would they like the house? The location? Would they be upset he hadn't involved them?

Craig rushed the final renovations so the house would be ready in time for his parents' wedding anniversary. He had even gone as far as hiring an interior designer and using Rose's connections to get the furniture there quickly. Rose ended up being the only person he could talk to about the house, and she was aware of every intimate detail and downfall.

Thankfully, his parents were excited when he told them he'd booked them a place for a getaway. They had no clue what was really happening, showing up early Saturday morning with their bags and bubbling with excitement.

As soon as they pulled up to the house, they both gushed over how beautiful it was, how peaceful they found the view, and how concerned they were he couldn't afford to rent it for an entire week.

"I know you're doing well, honey, but you shouldn't waste your money on us," his mom said, clutching her bag to her chest.

His dad wasn't as shy. "If the boy wants to treat us, he wants to treat us. He probably knows the owner."

Craig smiled. "I do."

"See?" his dad said. "I bet they gave you a great deal."

"You wouldn't believe it." Craig reached into his pocket and pulled out the keys. He'd ordered a custom keychain with their last name engraved on it.

He handed the keys to his mom, hoping she'd catch the hint, but she didn't notice. She was already bounding up to the door to open it.

Once inside, she threw the keys onto the counter and started touching everything. "Look at the color of these cabinets! They're gorgeous! What is that? Cream? Oh, and the copper pulls! I love it."

"That's real wood," his dad said, knocking on the door. "Nice and solid."

"Oh!" his mom exclaimed. "Look at that view! Can we go out there?"

"Of course," Craig said, opening the door to the wooden deck outside. He'd had glass railings installed so the sight of the trees and ocean were undisturbed.

His parents walked through the door and he followed them outside.

"Now *this* is incredible," his mom said, shaking her head. "Just breathtaking. It feels like the whales could swim by at any moment!"

Craig couldn't take it anymore. His mom was still clutching the keys in her hand, the keychain going completely unnoticed. He reached for the keys, holding them up. "Mom, did you see this?"

She took the keys back. "It's an orca keychain! So cute." She paused, squinting at the *Mitchell* engraved on the whale's tail. "Craig. *No!*"

He grinned. "Yes."

"Is this your house? Honey, it's stunning."

He shook his head. "No, it's not mine."

"You got your name on the keys." His dad had popped his reading glasses on, and they sat crooked on his face.

"It's not mine," Craig said. "It's yours."

His mom's mouth fell open and she froze.

His dad let out a whoop. "Are you kidding me?"

"I'm not kidding." Craig laughed. "Welcome home."

After some cheering and exclaiming, they went back inside, and Craig pulled a bottle of champagne out of the fridge. By the time he got a glass into his mom's hand, she was able to speak again.

Sort of. She kept repeating the phrase: "This is too much!"

"It's about the right size for us," his dad said with a shrug. "I don't love the color of the hardwoods..."

Craig jumped on his comment. "You don't? Last year you said you loved the hardwoods you saw at–"

He laughed. "I'm just pulling your leg. They're beautiful. Everything is just unbelievable."

Ah, good old Dad.

Craig laughed. "I'm glad."

An hour later, Craig was busy showing his dad everything about utilities – the furnace, the electrical box upgraded for the jacuzzi, the gas shut off – when his mom yelled out.

"Boys! Someone's here! I think it's a gardener?"

Craig stopped what he was doing and walked toward the kitchen. He hadn't gotten around to hiring a gardener.

When he reached the kitchen window and peered out, he caught sight of someone kneeling, pulling weeds. He stared for a moment until she turned and he saw her face.

Rose.

His stomach dropped. "That's not a gardener, it's my friend. I mean, technically she's one of my employees. Rose. She's the matchmaker."

"The matchmaker!" His mom put her hands on her hips. "I've wanted to meet her."

At that moment, as the three of them peered out the window like a trio of meerkats, Rose saw them and pushed up the brim of her hat. She smiled.

"Should we let her in or keep watching her?" his dad said with a laugh.

"I'll get the door," Craig said, rushing outside and making sure to shut it behind him. "Hi, ma'am. Can I help you with something?"

She took off a gardening glove and hid her face behind her hand. "I'm sorry. I thought they were coming tomorrow! I knew you were trying to get this ready for your parents and–" She stopped talking. "Oh. Hi."

Craig turned to see both of his parents standing in the doorway, smiling like fools.

Well, this was happening. "Rose, I'd like you to meet my parents."

"It's nice to meet you!" his mother yelled, waving. "Come in. Have some champagne. This is our house!"

Rose laughed. "I know! It's beautiful. Congratulations."

"Please, come in," his dad said, stepping aside. He caught Craig's eye and winked.

Oh dear. His dad was in too playful a mood for this meeting. "I'm sure she's busy," Craig said.

They ignored him, instead sweeping Rose inside before he could do anything to stop them.

"I know Craig was apprehensive you might not like the house," Rose said, accepting a glass of champagne. "It seems like the debut has gone well, though?"

"I can't get over the shock," his mom said. "But yes, we love it!"

"It's about time he did something for us," his dad said with a laugh.

His mom ignored her husband and focused on Rose. "Craig tells me you're a matchmaker. How did you get into that line of business?"

"Well," she smiled. "Craig convinced me."

He nodded. "I did, and it's the best business decision I've made in a decade."

"Are you single?" his mom asked.

Great, the two of them were going to work together on this.

Time to change the subject. Craig loudly cleared his throat. "You guys remember The Grand Madrona Hotel?"

His dad set his champagne glass down. "It was the first place I stayed when I came to the island. I haven't been there in twenty years."

"Rose's mom owns it now," Craig said brightly.

Rose nodded. "Yes, she does! It's just a beautiful place. She's been fixing it up with her husband, Chip."

"I would love to see it," his dad said. "Are there still those little madronas out front?"

"Yes, but they're not little anymore," Rose said. "My mom just started a new high tea service on the weekends."

His mom gasped. "I would *love* to go to a high tea. Do you think there are any openings today?"

"Uh," Craig stammered, "I'm sure they're booked."

"I'm sure we're not," Rose said. "Come on over. I'll give you the grand tour!"

There was no way for him to stop it, and further, he wasn't sure he wanted to. Yes, his dad was being pushy, but his mom was excited, and it gave him an excuse to spend more time with Rose.

Within minutes, they were walking out to their cars, Craig trailing behind with his dad.

"So, Dad, I bet you didn't expect to get a house today," he said, grinning.

"No. It's amazing. Really, it is." His dad bumped him in the arm. "If only there was something I could do to pay you back."

Before Craig could respond, he hopped into the driver's seat and shut the door. Craig reached for the backseat just as the locks clicked shut.

His dad rolled down the window. "Why don't you ride with your friend?"

"*Dad!*" He lowered his voice. "Let me in."

His dad couldn't contain his glee. "Bet you didn't think you'd be going on a double date with your parents today. See you there!"

Chapter Twenty

The turnout for their second high tea was underwhelming, but Claire wasn't upset by it. It was the offseason, after all, and it gave them time to perfect the tea service before boatloads of tourists returned in the summer.

Besides, it was such a fun experience, and it gave her an excuse to have the girls at the hotel, something she always relished.

Lucy insisted on serving as quality control, and Lillian was happy to tag along. Rose was going to stop by, too, fitting them into her ever-packed schedule.

"Good news," Claire said, rejoining the table. The tea had just arrived and each of them had their own teapot. Claire had selected the black currant tea, Lucy the pomegranate oolong, and Lillian the lemon ginger.

"Is Rose coming?" Lucy asked. "I can't keep track of her anymore."

Claire nodded. "Not only is she coming, but she's also bringing her boss, Craig, and his parents."

"That's *three* paying customers," Lillian said, raising her eyebrows at Lucy. "Not bad. Rose might be our new recruitment officer."

"Recruitment isn't my department," Lucy hissed. "I'm quality control! And I have to say, there was lipstick on my teacup."

Claire gasped. "Really? That's terrible!"

The teacups were made of fine bone china and had to be hand washed. It was a new task for the kitchen staff, and she'd worried it would be too much.

"It's *your* lipstick." Lillian pointed at the cup. "Look at the color. It's your coral passionfruit whatever."

"Oh." Lucy frowned. "You're right. Okay, the cups were clean. Nothing to worry about."

That was a relief. They could always pivot to cheaper, dishwasher-safe teacups, but these were beautiful. She and the girls had debated what to order for weeks, finally deciding on two designs.

The first, her favorite, had a cuckoo bird and flowers, gold lining the rim. The ones Lucy insisted on were light pink with delicate roses all around, gold painted on the leaves.

"Craig's parents are moving here." Lillian delicately set the silver strainer on her cup and poured out a portion of tea. "From what Rose told me, Craig got a house for them as a surprise."

"I can't imagine that big of a surprise." Claire shook her head. "I don't do well with surprises."

"You had enough of a surprise when you adopted us," Lucy said. "Luckily, now the only surprise you have to deal with is one of us getting arrested."

Claire laughed. "There *has* been a lot of that recently. It must be the island."

"I blame Lucy," Lillian said. "She's at the center of all of the incidents."

"Can't argue there." Lucy set down her teacup and when she looked up, her expression brightened. "There they are!" She dropped her voice. "Wait. Is that Craig? Rose didn't tell us he was cute."

Lillian turned around and Lucy whispered, "Don't look at him now. You're making it obvious we're talking about him."

"It's too late," Lillian said in a hushed voice. "You're right. Very cute. Why didn't she mention it?"

Claire suppressed a smile. Whatever Rose's reasoning, the cat was out of the bag now.

She stood from her seat to greet them and gave Rose a hug. "Hi, honey!"

"Hey, Mom," Rose said. "This is Craig, and these are his parents, Mr. and Mrs. Mitchell."

Craig's mom stuck out her hand. "Please, it's Denise and Leroy."

"Nice to meet you."

"Thanks for having us," Leroy said. He stood back, his eyes tracing the corners of the room. "It's incredible what you've done with the place. I remember it looking a bit run down. Now it's stunning."

Claire couldn't help but smile. "Thank you. Would you like to try our high tea? We can move to a bigger table and sit together?"

"And maybe afterwards we can give them a tour?" Rose asked.

"Of course!"

Lucy and Lillian gathered the teapots and cups and moved to a table large enough for all of them. The waiter came over and handed out menus, and it seemed like Denise couldn't be more delighted by the choices, pointing and asking about every other one.

"I actually had quite a bit of help setting this up," Claire explained. "My friend Margie lives on San Juan Island, and she introduced me to a woman who ran a tea shop there."

"Margie knows a tea lady?" Lucy mused.

"Margie knows everyone," Lillian said with a smile.

"Her name is Patty, and she's been so helpful," Claire said. "It doesn't seem like she does it much anymore, but she's so knowledgeable."

"What you've set up here is just divine," Denise said, grinning. "I can't wait to see what comes next!"

They put in their orders just as the first three-tiered stands arrived. There were cucumber sandwiches with pimento cheese, smoked salmon with lemon butter on crostini, vanilla and poppy seed scones, and an assortment of their finest desserts – lemon macarons with mint, strawberry cheesecake with shortbread crust, and raspberry tartlets.

"I was nervous about the macarons, but our pastry chef rose to the challenge," Claire said, admiring the display. There was something charming about the little sandwiches and tiny sweets that she couldn't get enough of. "You wouldn't believe it, but there aren't many places to get high tea on the island."

"No?" Denise laughed. "It looks incredible. I can promise we'll be regular customers."

Claire beamed. "We're happy to have you!"

Lucy reached forward and took a cucumber sandwich. "Did Craig show you your surprise yet?"

Lillian elbowed her. "*Lucy!*"

"What?" She stuffed the sandwich in her mouth and flashed a smile.

Denise took a macaron. "Yes, he did." She looked at him and her face lit up. "It's a dream come true. I still can't believe it."

"It's a small thank you for all you've done for me," Craig said simply.

"You did it all yourself, son," Leroy said. "We just tried to support you."

What a sweet family. Claire couldn't take it. "You must be so proud of him."

"Well, sure," Leroy laughed. "But we don't want to give him a big head, so don't tell him."

Denise swatted him in the shoulder. "We are *so* proud." She turned to Claire. "But *you* must be so proud of Rose! All I ever hear from Craig is how amazing she is and how much she's done for the company and how she's turned things around."

"We should actually thank Rose for the house," Leroy quipped. "It looks like she's the only one doing any work at that place."

Craig laughed. "I try to get in my one day of work a month."

The table erupted into laughter. The only one who wasn't laughing was Rose.

"That's not true!" she said. "Craig works tirelessly. The employees all love him, and he's always available to help. He is the best boss I've ever had."

"You're the best employee I've ever had," Craig said.

Lucy, whom Claire thought had been too quiet until now, set down her teacup. "Aren't you two just *the best*? Perfect, really."

Lillian started coughing and Lucy pounded her on the back. "Sorry," Lillian said. "Inhaled part of my scone."

Claire shot them a look, which both girls avoided. "Don't be jealous," Claire said. "I'm proud of all three of you."

"But mostly me," Rose said, holding up a finger.

Everyone laughed, and Claire decided it was best to head off whatever Lucy was edging toward, changing the topic to the renovations at the hotel.

As soon as everyone was done eating, Claire stood. "How about that tour?"

Craig had apparently been waiting for the invitation and jumped from his seat. "Yes, let's go."

"Rose," Lucy said, "I thought *you* were going to give the tour? You are *perfect* for it."

Claire shrugged. "I don't mind."

"You need to stay, Rose. I need to talk to you." Lillian smiled. "Sister business."

Rose looked up at the Mitchells and smiled. "I'll let you have your family time. Enjoy the tour!"

Lucy started to say something, but abruptly stopped when Lillian delivered a swift and obvious kick under the table.

"Let's start in the lobby," Claire announced, leading her guests away before Lucy got another chance to speak. She shot her one last look before taking the Mitchells through the door and back into the lobby.

Chapter Twenty-one

Rose waited until her guests disappeared from sight to kick off an argument with her sisters.

"What was that all about?" she demanded. "You two are acting like a pair of quarreling cats."

"A pair of quarreling cats," Lucy repeated. "Try saying that five times fast."

"A pair of quarreling cats," Lillian parroted.

Rose let out a huff. "Stop it!"

"I'm sorry." Lucy turned to her, arms crossed. "Are you feeling *left out?*"

Rose rolled her eyes. "Lucy. If you have something to say, just say it. I don't know what you're hinting at."

"Fine." She leaned in. "Why didn't you tell us you had a thing going on with Craig?"

"What?" She pulled back. "We don't have a *thing* going on."

"Don't lie to me, Rose!" Lucy pointed a finger. "I'm not an idiot. First, he brings you to meet his parents, then the two of you are going on and on and on about how perfect you think each other are."

That was not at *all* what had happened. "He didn't bring me to meet his parents. I stopped by the house to pull a few weeds because I didn't realize–"

"You were pulling weeds for him?" Lucy stared at her, her mouth open. "By my calculations, that means you've been dating him in secret for, what, like a year?"

"I haven't even known him for a year," Rose said.

"I guess you move fast."

"Okay, okay." Lillian put her hands up. "You can't attack her like this. She won't tell us anything if you keep being aggressive."

"There's nothing to tell," Rose insisted. "He's my boss, a great boss, and yeah, I pulled some weeds when his parents were there and...it's nothing."

Lucy and Lillian exchanged glances.

Rose sighed. "What."

Lucy started to speak, but Lillian beat her to it. "I'm not saying this to be mean or anything, but it doesn't seem like nothing."

"Yeah, it seems like he's in love with you," Lucy blurted out.

Rose looked at Lillian, fully expecting her to be on her side, but instead was met with a furrowed brow. "You can't believe her! That's ridiculous. He's not in love with me."

"He does seem quite fond of you," Lillian said.

"He looks at you with these big puppy eyes and laughs at everything you say," Lucy added.

"Craig is a supportive boss. There's nothing more." She sat back, waiting for them to argue, but they stared at her in silence. She went on. "I'm getting dinner with Greg on Tuesday."

"Craig?" Lucy tapped her ear. "Craig, the man who thinks you're special and funny and wonderful?"

"*Greg*," Rose said, "who, according to the internet, is no longer engaged."

Lillian groaned. "I was hoping you'd forgotten about him."

"*I* was hoping you wouldn't notice the engagement had been called off," Lucy said.

She loved her sisters, but they were *beyond* annoying today. "I told both of you that Greg and I are finally hitting our stride. You chose not to believe it and instead made up this fantasy about Craig." She stood and straightened her posture. "I will be going now. I am *very* busy and important."

Lucy laughed. "See you at home in twenty minutes."

She chose to ignore that comment, even if it was right.

~

Her sisters didn't mention Craig for the rest of the weekend, and Rose flew into Seattle on Tuesday. Their comments made her feel a bit weird, especially because she hadn't told anyone about the unwelcome feelings she sometimes maybe felt for him, and it made her wonder if they'd seen something she hadn't.

But no. It couldn't be. She *maybe* had gotten a *little* infatuated with her boss, what was the big deal? He was nice and handsome and successful. Anyone with a pulse might feel a little fluttery under his gaze. It didn't mean anything. It was nothing, nothing at all.

Greg. Now Greg was something. They were finally going to have the storybook ending to their love story. This was the moment it would all come together for them. They were finally coming into their own.

She left work early to get ready for her date with Greg. She had a couple of ideas for outfits and ended up happy with how her look turned out. Though she still hadn't lost the weight she wanted to lose, somehow her life still seemed to be going in the right direction.

It was genuinely surprising to her. For years, she'd been frustrated with her weight and told herself she would start living and enjoying life *after* she lost it.

Rose stared at herself in the mirror. The weight was there, but somehow, she was still happy. She was living her life; she was doing all of the things she thought she never could. She was going to meet up with Greg, and he'd look into her eyes and tell her how much she meant to him, and maybe even kiss her.

It was perfect. Well, almost. There was one problem. Her hands wouldn't stop sweating.

It was absurd. Everything was slipping out of her hands – her hair straightener, her eyeshadow (which fell to the ground and shattered into a million chalky pieces), even her phone as she typed a message to Lucy accusing her of slipping a sabotage herb into her water.

"I don't have sweat-causing herbs," Lucy wrote back. "But that sounds really funny, so I will look into it. Send Craig my love!"

Rose didn't dignify her purposeful name confusion with a response.

All the way to the restaurant, she kept shoving her hands into her coat pockets and drying them on the paper towels she'd hidden inside, terrified Greg would recoil at her cold, sweaty touch and set them back another year.

She was the first one to the restaurant and sat at the table, coat still on. Greg was a few minutes late, floating into her view as though walking on a cloud.

Rose stood and wiped her hands a final time. "Hey!"

"Rose!" He put his arms out for a hug.

No handshake. Thank goodness. Rose wrapped her arms around him, the familiar feeling of his chest like an echo from the past. "It's *so* nice to see you."

"You look great," Greg said. "Tech life suits you."

She flashed a smile. "Thanks. You look good, too."

There was no ring on his finger. That was her favorite part.

They took their seats and he flagged down the waiter. "I'll take a Jack Daniels on the rocks. Rosie?"

She smiled. "Diet Coke, please."

The waiter walked off, and Greg leaned back. "So!"

"So!" She took a shaky breath. "How have you been?"

"Crazy busy. You wouldn't believe it."

She nodded. "Tell me about it."

"Ha!" Greg picked up his menu. "Yeah, so crazy."

In his silence, she realized he must've thought her "Tell me about it" was a cliché phrase, not that she actually wanted to know what had been keeping him so busy.

That was okay. She could steer the conversation. "I'm loving my job at SerenadeMe."

"Oh yeah." He looked up. "Have you gotten to work much with Barnabas? I hear he's a genius."

"Barney?" She combed her mind. "Hm, not so much. I mostly work with Craig Mitchell. Do you know him?"

Greg's eyes didn't leave the menu. "Haven't heard of him."

"Oh."

He didn't say anything else, so she took the chance to glance at the menu. Her appetite had washed away in the flood of her sweaty hands, so she decided to order the first thing that caught her eye.

The waiter returned with their drinks. "Are you ready to order?"

"I think so," Greg said. "I'll get the ribeye, rare, with broccolini and a side of sweet potato."

"And for you, miss?"

She looked up. "The Caesar salad, please."

He wrote this down, took their menus, and left.

"Looks like working in tech has you eating healthier." He laughed. "You've changed!"

Rose shifted in her seat. "Not really. I still love pizza."

His lips twisted into disgust. "How can you eat that garbage, Rose? It's so many carbs. I've been keto for a year and I'm loving it."

"You don't eat carbs now?" She sat back and crossed her arms. "This place is famous for their honey oat bread. It comes hot out of the oven with a blob of cinnamon butter."

He shook his head. "Don't need it."

"Guess it's all for me, then."

He set his menu down. "So, how did you end up at SerenadeMe? I never saw you working at a startup. It's kind of funny."

She frowned. "What's funny about it?"

"Oh, you know. You just...you're not one to take risks."

That was true of the *old* her, but Rose Woodson, PhD was a new woman.

She wanted him to see that. "I was offered an opportunity and I took it."

The waiter dropped off a basket of still-warm bread and she thanked him, immediately reaching for a slice. She slathered it with butter, and it glistened under the soft lighting.

"I hope they're not taking advantage of you," Greg said. "You're inexperienced and–"

"They're not taking advantage of me," Rose said, her mouth full of bread. "Why would you say that?"

He sighed. "I just know how things are. It's a tough business out there."

"Yeah, well, I'm doing fine." She buttered another slice of bread and took a bite. "Maybe you should worry about yourself."

He put his hands up. "Hey, I'm just trying to be helpful."

Rose cleared her throat. There was no need to get her feathers ruffled. "Sorry, it's just all new. How have you been? How's work?"

"Amazing. My stock portfolio has never been happier."

He talked for twenty minutes about his role at the company, how much he'd grown, and how much he loved it. "It comes at a cost, though." Greg scratched his eyebrow with his finger. "I don't know if you knew this, but I got engaged."

"You did?" Rose feigned a surprised face as best she could, even going as far to touch a hand to her chest. "Congratulations!"

He shook his head. "Please. It's already over. I just couldn't..." He let out a breath. "...see myself with her, you know?"

Rose nodded. "Yeah."

"Sometimes I just...I wonder. You know? What could've happened between us. You and me. Greg and Rose, star-crossed lovers."

Her heart took off like a balloon. "I wonder sometimes, too."

"I feel like we never got it right, you know? I miss you. I do."

The balloon in her chest was going to carry her away if she didn't reel it in. All she could manage to say was, "Yeah."

He smiled, nodding. "Maybe we could, I don't know, spend some time together? I feel like I need you in my life again. And maybe you need me as your mentor."

The little balloon deflated. "A mentor?"

"Yeah, I mean, you're obviously very intuitive. You're making friends, but you can always use another one, right? Maybe I can advise you on career moves and you can help me too. Introduce me to people."

Their entrées arrived. Her salad looked decadent in its over-sized bowl, peppered with cheese and mounded with croutons. Underneath, the lettuce was chopped and torn. Chaos no matter how they tried to dress it up.

She looked away. "Introduce you to people like...Barnabas?"

"Sure." He shrugged. "If you think we'd click. It could be fun, you know? Like the old days. You and me against the world."

She forced a smile. "Huh. Yeah."

"I mean, I'm not ready to commit to anything, obviously. Getting out of an engagement was rough."

"I bet it was." Rose kept her eyes on her salad.

"But I have to say, Rosie, I just feel myself pulled back to you. Don't you feel it? We're always in each other's orbits."

She looked up, staring into his golden-brown eyes, searching.

What was she looking for? She'd waited for this moment. Meditated on it, dreamed of it. And yet? Why did it feel like there was nothing there?

"I don't know."

"Aw, come on. We're free spirits, both of us."

Rose picked up a crouton with her fingers and loudly chewed it. "I'm not really a free spirit, Greg. I'm kind of the opposite."

"That's why I *need* you in my life. To give me direction. To give me hope!"

She took a sip of her soda. "My roster for clients is full, actually."

He laughed and shook his head. "Good old Rose. You always know how to cheer me up."

"Good old Greg," she said, grabbing another piece of bread. "You never change."

Chapter Twenty-two

With the house renovation completed and his parents slowly moving to the island, Craig was able to shift his full focus to his next project: finding a new buyer for SerenadeMe.

It was no easy task. Not only would the board have to approve of the person, but the buyer would also need to outbid Brett. Craig had to be tight-lipped during his search, doing most of his poking and prodding through friends and acquaintances who could be trusted to keep quiet.

The only person who knew what Craig was up to was Barney, and while he supported Craig's efforts, he wasn't able to help. He said he felt like he was "one step away" from getting on a boat and floating away. The best he could do was introduce Craig to a few people.

After three weeks, Craig thought he might have something. He flew out to San Francisco and met with one of Barney's old friends, Phoenix.

The guy was a classic startup workaholic, much like Barney. He'd created an extremely successful image editing software company over the course of a decade. Four years ago, he sold it off, hoping to find happiness in retirement.

"My life has been empty ever since," he confessed, sitting pool-side at his sprawling mansion. "There's no hustle in my life. No one counting on me. Nothing matters."

Craig could empathize. "I think I'd be the same way. Barney can't wait to leave, but I'm not so sure. I love what we do. Slowing down might be nice, but walking away entirely? I wouldn't know where to go."

They spent hours talking about the ups and downs of business, and Phoenix was fascinated with the story of SerenadeMe. As the day progressed, however, the majority of his questions were about Rose.

"I'll be honest," Phoenix said. "I like to keep up on what Barney's doing, and I read that story in the paper. It's interesting, but...I'm not sure about the matchmaker thing."

Craig laughed. "Why? Matchmaking is an ancient art. Parents have been doing it for their children for centuries."

"The goal then was to join their farms, not to find love," Phoenix countered. "How can this matchmaker work better than your algorithm? It seems too woo-woo for me."

"You trust a computer to match people, but not a person?"

Phoenix paused, thinking on this, and then said, "Yeah. I do. The computer has data. The person just had experience, and a limited lifetime's worth at that."

"She uses the algorithm, but she improves on it. Brings in a human element, makes people face whatever lies they've been telling themselves."

At that point, they'd been talking for over six hours – the span of lunch, after lunch drinks, dinner, and dessert.

Craig didn't feel the need to hold back. "Rose is incredible. She's the type of person you dream of when you start a company."

Phoenix raised an eyebrow. "A unicorn?"

That was one way to think of her. "Honestly, yeah. We're thinking about having her train more matchmakers so we can expand, but I find it hard to believe anyone can be as good as she is."

"Then it's not scalable."

He shook his head. "It might not be."

The twinkling lights flickered above the pool and reflected in Phoenix's eyes. "I love a challenge."

"Not a challenge." He laughed. "It really might be impossible to replicate her. She's amazing. Rose is...she's everything."

Craig stopped and cleared his throat. Perhaps he'd said too much.

Luckily, Phoenix didn't seem to notice. He was on a high. "I don't know if I buy her schtick yet, but I'm excited, and that's something I haven't felt in months. Years, maybe. It sounds like a great place to be. I'm going to meet with my accountant and talk numbers. I want in."

"Yeah?" Craig couldn't stop smiling. "That would be incredible. I think I'd actually be happy selling to you."

A laugh burst from Phoenix and he shook his head. "You're terribly straightforward, do you know that?"

He shrugged. Once he might've agreed, but now, with all the hidden thoughts he had about Rose... "Yeah, you could say that."

On his flight back home, Craig got a message from Phoenix. "You know," he wrote, "you could stay on as COO. I think we'd work well together."

That sealed it. Phoenix was the perfect fit. He didn't *need* a job or a company; he was coming to SerenadeMe because of a genuine interest. Best of all, he wasn't a creep.

There was still a lot of work to be done; in Craig's case, convincing the board that this was the right move. His flight got him back in time for a board meeting the next morning, but as giddy as he was, he couldn't bring anything up about Phoenix yet.

The agenda had already been set and he wasn't going to try to change the focus. That week, it was all about Rose.

She had been at the company for nearly three months and had matched nineteen people. All but one were happy with their match, and the one who hadn't been happy was thrilled with their rematch.

Her results were incredible, and Barney had asked her to make a presentation to the board. She was going to blow them away.

He meant to tell her that – via text, or with an email – but he couldn't find the words, so instead, he showed up early to the conference room and hoped to catch her alone.

Barney was already there, coffee in hand. "Hey. I heard you and Phoenix hit it off."

Craig took a seat next to him at the long, shining table. "We did. Maybe I'm being tricked. He can't be as nice as he seems."

"No, that's actually how he is. The company buyout almost killed him. Bunch of guys in suits drove him away." Barney sighed. "One sympathizes."

Craig laughed and patted him on the back. "Are you doing okay?"

"Yeah, yeah." He shook his head and smiled. "I'm being dramatic. I can see the light at the end of the tunnel." He dropped his voice. "I feel guilty, but I'm not going to miss this place at all."

Before he could say anything, Rose walked in. "Good morning, fellas."

She had her laptop tucked under her arm and a bright green drink in her hand.

"You're looking chipper today," Barney said. "Are you ready for this?"

"I was born ready!" She set her laptop down, but when her eyes met Craig's, her smile faded.

His heart sank.

It seemed like ever since their high tea at the hotel, she'd been avoiding him. This all but confirmed it.

"Barney," she said, eyes focused on her laptop, "have you ever been contacted by a guy named Greg Henley?"

Barney leaned back and crossed his arms over his chest. "The name sounds familiar. Why?"

Because it was her ex-boyfriend. Or maybe her current boyfriend and they'd finally gotten back together like she'd said they would. Maybe that was why she didn't want to talk to

Craig. He'd gotten too friendly, too obvious, the boss who was in love with one of his employees.

"He's an old friend. We used to date." She stopped what she was doing and looked up, keeping her eyes on Barney. "I met up with him for dinner the other day and it seemed like all he wanted to do was talk about you."

That snake! How dare he try to use Rose to get to Barney!

Craig could feel the heat rising in his chest. There were a dozen things he wanted to say, but he was so angry, all he could manage was, "You're kidding."

Barney just laughed. "I don't know what it is, but I tend to attract tech bro admirers."

"Brewpies," Craig interjected. "Bro-groupies."

"They can get creepy." He sighed. "They'll never find me on my boat."

Rose cocked her head to the side. "What boat?"

"The boat I'm going to live on when we sell this company." He clapped his hands together. "I'm counting on you, Rose. You keep driving up that stock price and getting us in the paper and I'll be in the middle of the Pacific by Christmas."

She reached out her hand and offered a handshake. "Deal."

Barney laughed and they shook hands. A moment later, Rose started setting up her presentation. "I'm glad to know you don't want anything to do with Greg, either."

Either?

Craig had to hide his face. The rest of the board members began filtering in, and Barney introduced Rose to each member one by one.

That was what Craig would have done, had he been able to speak. Instead, he sat and tried to look busy, clicking things mindlessly on his phone.

All the while, his mind spun. Could it be true? Was Rose done with her ill-fated ex? Had she decided to move on?

There were no answers during the meeting. Instead, there was just Rose, standing at the front of the room in her light blue suit, her hair catching the shine from the projector. She was stunning. It wasn't just the beautiful PowerPoint she'd put together, wowing the board—it was *her*. She glowed.

When she finished and the meeting adjourned, Barney was the first one to stand, shaking her hand and whispering, "You're a star."

The best Craig could do was nod and say, "Good job."

Rose smiled, thanking him, and walked out the door. Craig watched her leave, then felt a hand on his shoulder.

Barney. "Is there something you need to tell me?"

He shook his head. "I don't think so."

"It seems like you're angry today. Or stressed out. Are you not happy with Rose anymore? Please tell me it's not that."

Craig raised his eyebrows. "No. She's amazing. She's the reason we're going to be able to sell. She's – Rose is everything for this place."

"Oh." Barney took a step back. His eyes widened. "*Oh.*"

Crap. He should've stuck to not speaking. It was surprising it had taken Barney this long to catch on, actually.

Craig looked over his shoulder and lowered his voice. "Don't."

"I'm not going to say anything. I'm not going near that with a ten-foot pole. You can talk to HR about your feelings."

Craig scoffed. "Thanks."

"Good luck, man." He smiled. "Really."

He was going to need it.

Chapter Twenty-three

Her due diligence was done. Rose could respond to Greg's pathetic follow-up email about Barney with honesty.

She got back to her office and typed out her reply. "He says he doesn't know you. Sorry." She was about to hit send, then added, "Good luck finding someone to mentor!"

The email went off into the world, and that was the end of it. No more waiting to meet with him. No more hoping he was thinking of her. No more delusion.

Rose thought it would be different to turn down his weak proposal – freeing, in a way – but it wasn't that simple.

All these years, she'd been a fool. How could she have believed he was a wonderful person and they would work things out in the end, that all they needed was time?

He'd popped into her life and tried to act like a friend, only confusing her further. It let her keep thinking they'd end up together.

Despite thinking exclusively about himself all the time, Greg still didn't know what he wanted, and he *still* couldn't settle down. Rose finally saw him for what he was: the same sad, confused boy he'd been when they graduated from college.

Still, it wasn't his fault. She'd created this hallucination of their love all on her own. For whatever reason, she'd preferred the comfort of that fantasy to reality.

As painful as it was to realize she'd wasted all those years, she took solace in the fact that it was over and it had ended on her terms. This was the first day of the rest of her life.

~

Rose hung around the office for the rest of the week. Partially she wanted to look good to whatever board members were around, now that they knew her face, but a less honest part of herself was hoping Craig would come in to talk to her.

She'd been so distracted by Greg that she missed the person right in front of her, the one she could spend hours talking to, the one who made her laugh. The one who had seen something in her – something *real*, not like Greg, who only saw what she could do for him.

If only he'd show up in her office. If only he'd give her some hint of how he felt or what he thought.

Unfortunately, she wasn't that lucky. Craig was nowhere to be found. He mentioned he was looking for another buyer, so she assumed he was busy with that and not busy avoiding her. He'd told her to go forward with finding a match for Brett, too, saying it was important not to spook him or let him onto the fact that he was about to lose his chance to buy the company.

There were some lovely candidates for Brett – women closer to his age, which was good – but Rose thought they were *too* lovely, especially for him. It felt wrong to subject any woman to his boorishness.

Mid-week, Rose changed her tactics and started looking for someone who wouldn't mind dating a brute in exchange for material comfort. To her surprise, she couldn't find anyone like that. The whole "gold digger" stereotype wasn't proving to be real.

Friday afternoon, Rose gave up waiting on Craig and flew back to the island. Lucy had planned a girls' night where they would watch old movies, binge their favorite candy, and paint their nails.

Rose was looking forward to it. She felt guilty about how busy she'd been, and she thought showing up with a bag full of Reese's Pieces would buy her forgiveness.

The candy did nothing. As soon as she walked in the door, Lucy started.

"Busy kissing Craig all week?" she asked. "Or was it Greg?"

Rose groaned and flopped onto the couch. "It wasn't Greg."

"What happened?" Lillian set down a tray with three mugs of hot chocolate, then slid into the seat next to her. "I thought you said dinner with him was nice."

"It was nice seeing him, and it was nice talking to him. I got clarity about our relationship."

Lucy crossed her arms. "What relationship?"

"*Lucy!*" Lillian shook her head and snatched away a bag of Twizzlers. "Why do I have to yell at you all the time?"

Lucy stuck out her tongue.

"It's fine." Rose waved a hand. "Lucy was right about him."

Her mouth popped open. "I was?"

"He's the same person, and not in a good way. He broke up with his fiancée because he couldn't decide what he wanted. And she was perfect!"

Lucy scrunched her forehead. "She kind of was."

"He still wasn't happy with her." Rose sighed. "He sort of tried to get back with me."

Lillian gasped, immediately covering her mouth with her hand. "What did you say?"

"Nothing." Rose stared at the floor. "It was so disappointing. I wasn't excited. He's just...not who I thought he was."

Lucy picked up the tray of mugs and handed them each one. "I say we raise a hot chocolate toast to Rose *finally* waking up and kicking that loser out of her life."

"I'm sorry," Lillian said. "I know this must be hard for you."

"I'm not even upset about Greg. That's the weird thing." Rose looked at Lucy, who was still cheerfully waiting for them to raise their mugs.

Rose obliged. "To Lucy, for being right about Craig, too."

They clinked mugs, and Lucy was mid-swig when she started coughing and choking. "Wait, what? Craig's in love with you?"

Rose covered her eyes. "I think it's the other way around."

"*You're* in love? With your *boss*?" A smile spread across Lillian's face. "You are turning into Lucy."

Lucy let out a bellowing laugh. "I forgot I did that. That was bad."

"*This* is bad," Rose said. "I can't be in love with him. I've been lying to him from the moment I met him. It's a disaster."

"He's way cuter than Greg," Lucy said. "And much more successful. Your tastes are really maturing."

Rose took another sip, savoring the taste of cocoa. "He's so much more than Greg. So much kinder..."

"So maybe he'll be understanding?" Lillian suggested.

"I don't know." Rose sunk deeper into the couch. "He's used to people counting on him. His parents sent him away to this expensive school just as a little kid. That was *so* much pressure, but he delivered."

"I'm sure he's used to liars, then," Lucy said.

Lillian smacked her on the shoulder.

"No, she's right," Rose said. "I'm a liar. I wasn't a liar before this, but I told a big lie, and I kept telling it, so I'm a liar."

"Tell him the truth," Lillian said. "It's not easy, but it is simple."

"It's not that simple. Craig is..." Rose stuffed her mouth full of Reese's Pieces and tried to work out what she wanted to say. "He's like the opposite of Greg. He only thinks of other people. Not because he needs to use them – it's nothing like that. He doesn't use people. He seems to only depend on himself."

Lillian grimaced. "He doesn't let anyone in, does he."

She shook her head. "But for some reason, he let me in."

"All right, I see how it's pretty bad now." Lucy plopped down next to her. "You're in a pickle."

"I'm going to have to quit and move away. Start over as a new person," Rose said.

Lucy shook her head. "That's not going to work, because considering your history, you'll probably be in love with Craig for the next ten years."

Rose groaned. "I *know*."

"There's no way around it," Lucy said. "Lillian's right. You're a big girl. Tell him. You can do it."

"It's not just about him. If people find out I'm a fraud, it could halt the sale of the company, crash the stock price, ruin his life..."

"Tell him *after* the sale, and after wedding, then." Lucy laughed and took a Twizzler from Lillian, snapping it between her teeth.

There wasn't going to be a wedding. As kind and gentle as Craig was, he wouldn't be able to forgive her for this.

Would he?

If only she could find a way to protect the company. That way, the only thing she'd destroy was...his trust.

Rose rubbed her face with her hands. "What're we watching? I need to get my mind off what a mess I am."

Lucy tapped her chin. "I've got two cinematic masterpieces: *Clueless* and *The Silence of the Lambs.*"

Rose hated scary movies, but she'd hate seeing someone as clueless as her fall in love even more. "Bring on Hannibal Lecter."

Lillian shrieked. "I don't think I can stomach it."

"Shh," Lucy said, picking up the remote. "You're going to love it. Or be haunted with nightmares. I mean, I guess we'll see."

Rose smiled, settling into the couch and stuffing another handful of candy into her mouth.

She'd figure it out. Somehow.

Chapter Twenty-four

H is visit to the human resources department started as a mission in secrecy and ended as a lesson in management.

Craig had made an appointment with Sherry, the head of HR. He felt ridiculous even talking to her about asking Rose out. There was no way to be sure Rose *wanted* to go on a date with him, but he didn't want to even think about asking her unless he knew it would be okay with company policy.

Sherry would have the final word. She could tell him if his romantic daydreams were morally dubious and give him an excuse to delay or even chicken out entirely.

"I need to know what the process is for someone in the company who might want to start a relationship with someone else at the company," Craig said.

Sherry leaned back in her chair, pushing her glasses up the bridge of her nose. "Is this 'someone' in a position of power over the other 'someone?'"

"Yes."

She smiled. "Is that first someone *you?*"

There were no secrets in HR. Craig knew this, but still. He didn't like it. "Could be."

"You know you're not supposed to officially start a relationship until–"

He cut her off. "I was only *thinking* of asking her – I mean, someone – out. I don't even know if she'll say yes."

Sherry leaned in, her eyes bright. "Who's the lucky lady?"

Craig crossed his arms. "Is there a form I need to fill out?"

"Come on. Tell me who it is!"

Craig shook his head. "Can't."

She narrowed her eyes. "You know, I'm under no obligation to keep this conversation private. I can send an email to the entire female staff and ask who thinks they caught your eye. Might be an interesting experiment to see who responds."

"Sherry." He put his hands on her desk. "Can you *please* just tell me what I have to do?"

She waved a hand. "There's a form that both parties fill out saying you won't sue the company if you break up." She shrugged. "It's not a big deal."

He stood. "Thank you."

"Maybe I should start a betting pool with the rest of the office ladies about who you're going to ask out."

"Maybe I should be a scarier boss so you *don't* do that?" Craig said.

Sherry laughed. "Too late for that. Have a good day!" She paused. "Hope it's a romantic one!"

He shook his head and walked out the door. What a nightmare it was to be nice.

Despite the awkwardness, his spirits were high as he walked back to his office. Sherry had given him much better news than he expected. It actually seemed too easy to date people at the company. How many people were in relationships? How many had broken up? Was there a separate form for that?

Maybe when he was less annoyed with Sherry, he would go back and ask her.

He got back to his desk and saw he had a new email from Phoenix. He said he was ready to meet with the board and make an offer, but he also asked to meet Rose to see if she was "as amazing as foretold."

Hm. That could be touchy, too. Phoenix may not take his glowing recommendation as seriously when he found out they were dating.

If they ended up dating. There was no way to know what she'd say until he asked her.

If he asked her.

No, he was going to ask her. He was.

He had a plan. He would invite her to a pizza-making class, and at the end, tell her how he felt. Lay it all on the table. He'd considered adding pepperoni in the shape of a heart to his pizza, but decided it was too cheesy.

There didn't need to be theatrics. All that needed to happen was for him to tell her how wonderful she was, beautiful— not that that was the most important—funny, brilliant...

The truth was, when he looked back over the last few years, the best hours of his life were spent sitting and talking with her.

Craig pulled up the document on his computer where he'd typed out all these thoughts. He didn't want to have a speech, exactly, when he told her how he felt, but he wanted to have something coherent.

He was absorbed in the document, scanning what he'd put down, when he looked up and saw Rose standing in front of him.

It was if she'd stepped out of his mind. He gasped.

Rose put her hands up. "Sorry! I didn't mean to scare you. Is this a bad time?"

She was wearing the outfit she'd worn on her first day in the office – a black dress and a flowery blazer. For some reason, it was seared in his mind. At the time, he thought she'd be the answer to all the company's problems. If only he'd known...

"I've always got time for you," he said. "Please, have a seat. What's up?"

She took a few hurried steps and lowered herself into the seat across from him. "I don't think I can keep this up, Craig."

"Keep what up?" He cocked his head to the side. "Being the matchmaker?"

She bit her lip. "No, wait. I didn't want to start there. Let me start over." She sighed. "I'm worried because..."

Her voice trailed off, and Craig leapt in. "Don't be worried. I haven't had a chance to tell you everything about Phoenix, but he'd like to meet with you. I told him how incredible you are."

She winced. "That's nice."

"Not to scare you, but he has some doubts about match-making. I don't think it's a problem, because your numbers speak for themselves, but he's more comfortable with machines than people. You know the type."

She looked at her hands, and when she looked back up at him, her eyes looked glassy. "Craig."

Oh no. "It's really not a big deal, don't worry about–"

She cut him off. "I don't know how to tell you this because I love working here. Like, really love it. And...I like you. A lot."

Craig's throat was suddenly dry. He forced a swallow. "Are you breaking up with us?" he said with a weak laugh.

"No. Crap." She rubbed her forehead. "I don't know what to say first." Rose pressed her hands together, then stood up. "I thought I could just come in, do the work, make some money, and eventually I'd get fired."

He stood, too, and looked her in the eye. "I'm not going to fire you. Have you been talking to Sherry?"

"What? Who's Sherry?"

"Never mind." He cleared his throat. "Rose, you're a star employee."

She turned away from him and paced toward the door, then back. "I wasn't going to tell you this, but I have to now. I like you, Craig. Not just as a boss. I..." She looked down again and sighed.

It felt like a flock of butterflies hit him in the chest. "I've been looking for a way to tell you I feel the same way."

She put up a hand. "Please, let me finish." She sighed and put her hands on her hips. "I'm not who you think I am."

He stared at her, trying to process what she'd said. "Okay?"

"Do you remember that day at the news studio?"

He nodded, and she went on. "I was supposed to be on a different floor for a different interview. My name is Rose Woodley, and I'm an administrative assistant to the stars." She shook her head. "Just kidding. Not the stars. Mostly people who scream at me a lot."

His mind, slow as it was caught up in a tornado of magical butterflies, started to catch up to the conversation. "So you're not Rose Woodson..."

"They mistook me for her. They asked if I was there for an interview, and I said yes, because I was. Then they pulled me in front of the camera and I just started talking. I don't even remember what I said. Then your assistant came to get me, and you were so persistent–"

"You're not Rose Woodson?" He repeated, lowering himself into the nearest chair.

"No. I'm not."

He looked up at her. "Do you have a PhD in psychology?"

She shook her head. "I don't."

"You didn't write that book, did you?"

Rose shut her eyes and covered her face with her hands. "No, and I'm so sorry, because I love this job and I respect you so much and–"

"I've been going around the country telling everyone what an amazing psychologist you are."

She stared at him. "I know."

"The entire sale to Phoenix is based on me telling him you're marvelous, and vouching for you, and saying you're one of a kind."

"I *know*."

He could hear his voice getting louder, but he couldn't stop it. "There were news stories written about you! If they found out you lied your way into this job, it would ruin the credibility of the company, we would lose clients, we wouldn't be able to sell, and I'm pretty sure Barney would jump off a dock!"

"I know!" She yelled back. "This isn't what I wanted to happen."

He stared at her. It felt like he was looking at Rose, the woman he knew well and trusted.

But it wasn't Rose, not really. She was essentially a stranger. It was uncanny, and truth be told, he felt a little sick. "This isn't a game, Rose. These are people's livelihoods."

She started backing out of the room, her hand over her mouth. "I'm so sorry. I'm–"

She turned and disappeared through the door.

Chapter Twenty-five

C rying at work was in the top three of Rose's least
favorite activities. She hated that she was a crier. It'd
been this way since she was a kid, and though she'd gotten
much better about getting yelled at, tears could still surprise
her when she least wanted them to spring up.

Normally she could hold it together until she got to her
car, or at least to the bathroom. This time, however, it wasn't
holding.

Rose skirted out of Craig's office and kept her head down
on the way to grab her coat and purse. A few tears slipped out
as she waited for the elevator, but thankfully no one was there
to see them.

In the lobby, she picked up her pace, and once outside, she
broke into a run, tears streaming out of her eyes and dropping
off her cheeks in droves.

She ran for two blocks, until the tears slowed and her face
dried. Her lungs were on fire and she stopped, looking up
between the buildings. Rose had the urge to keep going, to
walk down street after street after street, to wander until the
sun set, until she was somewhere else, until *she* was someone
else.

But her shoes kept slipping off her heels and she was gasping for air, so instead, she called her sister.

"Hey, hey," Lillian said, answering after a few rings. "How's it going?"

"Lillian." Rose took a deep breath. "I told him."

"You did? Did you tell him everything?"

Rose could feel her lip starting to quiver. "Uh huh."

"What happened? Are you okay?"

Rose wanted to answer, but a sob swelled in her chest and burst through her mouth. "I don't know."

"Where are you? I'll come and pick you up."

"I don't know where I am." She looked around, blinking into the sunlight. "I mean, I'm in Seattle, but I ran away from the building. I don't think I've ever been this direction."

"Well, go and find a Starbucks, then send me your location. I'm in town for work today. I'll be there as soon as I can."

"Okay." Her eyes felt like they were spinning in her head, but that was one thing she could see – a Starbucks on the next block. "Should I get you anything?"

Lillian laughed. "No, it's okay. I'll be there soon. Hang tight!"

Rose put her phone back into her purse and took a deep breath before starting the slow march across the street.

Despite her theatrics, no one had stopped to look at her, which was a strange comfort, though it did make her feel more alone.

She opened the door to the coffee shop and walked into a comfortingly familiar scene. The smell of newly roasted beans surrounded her and pulled her in. People chatted in low voices and music played quietly in the background.

Calm. Coffee.

This was good. She could do this.

Rose got in line. Even though all her favorite drinks were on the menu for fall, she couldn't get into the spirit. She ordered a black coffee and took a seat in the corner.

Rose pulled out her phone and used the camera to see how terrible she looked after her cry-and-run.

Surprisingly, her makeup hadn't streaked much – just a bit of mascara under her eyes. She was able to wipe it away with a napkin. Worse were the blotches on her face, her skin's way of expressing its anger for her daring to exercise.

How had it all gone so badly? Why hadn't she planned what she was going to say?

When Rose woke up that morning, she had a pressure in her chest. It felt like if she didn't talk to Craig immediately, she'd never be able to. She'd have to keep up the lie forever, getting a fake PhD to drag around for the rest of her life.

She had visions of hanging the monstrosity in her office and bringing it to dinner parties. People would ask why the lettering looked funny and she'd tell them it was very old, like her and her education, and not to ask any more about it. Then she'd return home with Craig, a man who married her without ever knowing her real name or ever meeting her old college friends, because she had to fake all of that as well.

When she'd burst into Craig's office that morning and he'd met her with those kind eyes, she thought it would be okay. She thought she could tell him how she felt and it would work itself out. They would laugh about how silly she'd been, and he would say it was fine, *better* even, if she wasn't Rose Woodson, because Rose Woodley was enough.

That was the lie. That was the problem. Rose Woodley had never been enough. She'd never been smart or assertive enough to get a promotion. She'd never been tall or thin enough to enjoy the beach without hiding under a towel, lying that she didn't like to swim, that she didn't like the sun. To Greg she'd *never* been enough. He didn't know what he was looking for, what it'd take to settle down, but it wasn't her.

Why did she think this time was different? How could she have been so naïve?

It wasn't enough to ruin Craig's trust. Rose had to go and endanger the company, too. Lying about her education was one thing; getting a bunch of publicity as a fake expert was another.

Craig was right. If her lie got out, SerenadeMe would lose credibility. Investors would flee. Users would be appalled that an imposter was making matches and they'd run to companies that didn't lie to them, like Brett's.

Shudder.

All her lovely, cheerful coworkers – what would happen to them when SerenadeMe lost half of its users? When the stock price fell? When the board had to make cuts?

They'd get laid off, that's what. They'd be left to scramble for their next job, their next paycheck. Marriages would crack under the strain, and children would hear tense arguments through walls and slammed doors.

All because Rose had wanted to play pretend.

She wanted to crawl into a cave and disappear. Her breathing picked up and she felt the tears coming back, welling up in her chest, crashing out of her eyes. She was on the brink of losing it when the door opened and Lillian appeared.

She gave a little wave and a smile. Rose raised her hand and waved back.

Chapter Twenty-six

The skin under Rose's eyes was dark and shiny. She was completely unable to return Lillian's smile, her face sullen and pale.

Lillian rushed over and slipped into the seat across from her. "Hey! How are you doing?"

"Badly." Rose kept her eyes focused on the coffee cup in front of her, picking at the cardboard seam. There was no lid on the cup, half of the black coffee gone. "Are you going to get a drink?"

Lillian shook her head. "I'm fine. Unless you want something?"

"Could you get me a new identity? I messed mine up."

Lillian frowned and tapped a finger on her chin. "How about a pumpkin spice latte? Would that be a good start?"

Rose shrugged, so Lillian popped into line to get a latte for each of them. She also grabbed a pack of cookies, because cookies never hurt.

She sat back down and slid the drink across the table. "I got you extra whipped cream."

"Thanks."

"Do you want to tell me what happened?"

Rose shrugged. "Not really."

Lillian stayed quiet and opened the cookies. Rose reached across the table and took one. When she was finished chewing, she went into the entire story, going as far as to claim that SerenadeMe would collapse into a black hole because of her.

"I know you've been doing a good job and you're important," Lillian said gently, "but don't you think that's a little grandiose?"

"If Craig wasn't desperately trying to sell the company, no, but he is. Apparently, the new buyer was already leery of me. What's he going to think now?" She sighed, puffing out her cheeks. "He's going to walk away from the deal. Craig is going to have to fire me."

"He's not going to fire you."

"I'm pretty sure I'm already fired. I admitted to lying about my qualifications and my name. I literally couldn't have lied about more important things."

Okay, that was kind of bad, but now wasn't the time to dwell on it. "Just go and talk to him. I'll bet he's calmed down, and the two of you can come up with a plan to fix things."

"I don't think he'll ever speak to me again." Rose rubbed her face with her hands. "I know what I have to do."

Lillian set her drink down. "That sounds ominous."

"I need to convince Brett to buy the company. That's the only solution."

Ugh, Brett. Lillian didn't want Rose to have to talk to that guy again. "But he's ridiculous!"

"I know, and that's why it might work. If I make him feel like I like him, like it's a good idea...that he's getting a deal..."

"Rose," Lillian said slowly, "why would you need to make him think you like him?"

Rose continued mumbling to herself, her speed picking up. "He won't ask questions, he's too obtuse, and if he buys the company, no one has to know the truth. I'll train someone to replace me, then leave. Disappear. The company will be fine, no one will be the wiser..."

"You love this job, though. You can't quit."

Rose's eyes snapped into focus, as though she'd just remembered Lillian was there. "I *have* to quit. I don't want anyone to lose their livelihood because of me."

"That is not going to happen," Lillian said firmly.

"You don't understand how high the stakes are." She shook her head. "I never should've done this in the first place. I didn't belong in a company like this."

"That's not true!" Lillian leaned in and grabbed her hands. "It clearly didn't matter that you don't have a PhD. You were still amazing at matching people. That was all *you*, and you can't deny that."

There was silence while Rose stared straight ahead, her expression flat. "You should've seen the way he looked at me. I swear I felt my heart crack." She touched a hand to her chest and let out a long, heavy sigh. "I think he might've even said he liked me back. I ruined that, too."

This was too many problems muddled into one. Rose wasn't thinking clearly.

Lillian nudged a cup toward her. "You haven't even tried your drink yet."

Rose stared at the coffee cup. "I used to love pumpkin spice lattes."

"What do you mean *used* to?"

"When I was happy."

Lillian cracked a smile. "Rose."

She picked up the cup and swirled it in her hand. "What."

"I promise we'll find a way out of this. It's going to be okay."

She took a swig and set the cup down. "You're right. I'm going to call Brett and ask him on a date."

Lillian almost spit out a mouthful of coffee. *"What!"*

"That's the solution. I'm going to take him on a date and convince him I like him, then get him to buy the company as soon as possible."

"Rose! You can't do that."

She had her phone in her hand and her eyes narrowed. "Watch me."

Lillian sat back and took a sip of her drink. She had to change her tactics. Rose wasn't listening to her, and she wasn't going to be stopped.

But maybe she could be helped.

Chapter Twenty-seven

It was going to be a late night. Craig could accept that. What he couldn't accept was his state of mind.

While there was nothing more important than securing the future of the company, he couldn't focus. The walls of his office felt like a cage, trapping him with his anger and frustration.

His mind kept jumping back to the day he met Rose, how he'd practically chased her down the street. Begged her to work for him.

Was it his fault he'd hired her, or had she tricked him?

He changed gears, looking at minutes from board meetings, and ran into a copy of her presentation. It was impossible not to click through. He had been so excited, so convinced of her genius.

Was it all an illusion? Had he trusted the wrong person, hoped the wrong hopes? Whatever the story, the reporter who hung around the office would *love* to piece it together – how the COO tried to cover his feelings of inadequacy by coming up with the half-witted plan of hiring a matchmaker.

Someone to fix all their problems! A magical matchmaker! He might as well have hired a hypnotist. It would've worked on him because he wanted to believe. Because he was a rube.

Craig stood from his desk and went to look out the window. The sun had set not long ago, and the last hints of red lingered in the sky. He could see into the building across the street. Some offices were bright and warm, like beacons in the night, while others had fallen to darkness.

What would his office look like once he was fired? Who would they replace him with?

He turned away, back to his desk, determined to sell the company before anyone realized what he'd done. His best hope was Phoenix, who hadn't liked the idea of a matchmaker in the first place. Craig had nearly convinced him to accept Rose as an important part of the company. How hard would it be to change his mind again?

He was deep in thought, scribbling in a notebook, when his assistant Lydia walked in.

"Hey, Craig? There's someone here to see you. I found her wandering around the lobby."

"Right now?" He looked at his watch. "I thought you had gone home."

"You didn't seem well," she said, making a face. "I went to dinner and stopped back in case there was anything I could do to help you."

She was too good. She didn't deserve to lose her job because he was a failure. "That's nice of you, but I'm okay." He squinted at his computer screen, his eyes tense and strained. "Who is it? Can I send them away?"

Lydia laughed. "You're the boss, you can do whatever you want. It's Rose's sister – or, at least, that's who she said she was."

He tried to keep the surprise off his face but couldn't help raising his eyebrows. "Okay. I'll handle it. Please go home and have a good night."

"Thanks. You too!"

She disappeared and Lillian floated through the doorway, making Craig do a double take. He'd expected Lucy, and barely managed to sputter out a "Hi."

Lillian hesitated. "Can I come in?"

She was so polite he didn't dare refuse her. "Please."

She sat down, her hands folded in her lap. "I don't know if you remember me."

"I do. Lillian. It's nice to see you again." He paused. "I'm not sure why you're here."

"I need to talk to you about Rose."

"There's nothing to talk about." He stood, walking to the bookshelf and grabbing a random book, trying to look like he had a purpose. "I'm not sure what she told you–"

"She told me everything."

"Ah. Then you probably know more than I do."

She winced. "Rose made a mistake."

He tossed the book onto his desk and it landed with a louder thud than he'd intended, cutting her off.

"Sorry." He cleared his throat. "But no, Rose didn't make a mistake. A mistake would be getting phished in an email or leaving a mug in the sink for weeks. Rose lied about who she was – *what* she was." Craig stopped and took a deep breath. "And now I'm left picking up the pieces."

"She didn't do it on purpose!" Lillian's eyes flashed down, and she spoke again with a softer voice. "Lucy and I encouraged her to take the job. She wasn't going to. She was mortified after being mistaken for Dr. Woodson."

Craig interrupted. "Maybe I'll give the real Dr. Woodson a call and see if she'd like the job?"

A slight smile crossed her face. "I've already talked to her. I sent her an email explaining the situation, and she thinks the whole thing is really funny. She forgot she'd booked that interview. She's a sort of nutty professor type."

Who did Lillian think she was, contacting the real Rose Woodson before he'd thought to do it? "Rose is lucky she's not being sued. Either by Dr. Woodson or by us."

"Sued?" Lillian scrunched her eyebrows, a playful smile still dancing on her lips. "That's a bit drastic, don't you think? Sued for what?"

"For fraud. For lying." He sat down and picked up the book he didn't need. "She misrepresented her education and made us believe she was qualified when she wasn't."

"Except she obviously *was* qualified, because she made fantastic matches. She did all that programming, and she brought a bunch of good publicity to the company!"

Craig glanced at Lillian, then turned to his computer. "That's not the point."

Lillian sat back. "Then what is the point?"

"The point is," he said, looking up and locking eyes with Lillian, "integrity and honesty. And our company values." Or something. He didn't know how to put it into words. "She lied to us. To all of us, and it's damaging."

He clicked around on his computer, trying to find something to make him look busy. His email had a few unread messages; he'd start there.

"You have trouble trusting people." Lillian's voice was soft and nonjudgmental. She said it like she was observing the rain.

He sighed. "Don't try to pull a Rose and figure me out."

"I'm not trying to figure you out." She shook her head. "Rose told me about you. She told me how it was for you as a kid."

There it was. "I had a wonderful childhood," he said decidedly. "I had the best education possible, and it opened doors for me."

Lillian was unruffled by his stern tone. She stared at him for a moment, then said in a small voice, "It couldn't have been easy having to go to those expensive schools and be on your own."

He put his hands in his lap. "It was fine."

"That sort of thing can make it hard to get close to people. Hard to trust people."

He sighed. "It can."

"Rose – she's destroyed by this. She really is. It's completely out of character, and she truly, *truly* understands the weight of what it means to lose your trust."

But not to earn it in the first place, apparently.

This was getting far more uncomfortable than he wanted. "What does it matter?"

"Rose never meant to hurt you."

"Good for her." He'd recovered his normal speaking voice. He put his hands on his desk. "Is there anything else? I have a lot of work to do."

"She's in love with you, you know."

Craig laughed. "Sure she is."

"You don't believe me?" Lillian leaned forward. "Why do you think she confessed everything to you?"

He put his hands up. "Why does Rose do anything she does? She's a liar. There's no use in figuring her out."

"My sister is not a liar." Lillian said. "She fell in love with you and she had to tell you the truth. Even if it ruined everything."

"I hope she feels better, then." He turned to his computer screen, hoping she'd take the hint.

She did and stood. "I'm sorry." She got to the door and turned. "Just so you know, Rose is on a date right now."

His jaw tightened and he had to take a deep breath to release it. "That's nice."

"With Brett. She's throwing herself at his mercy, hoping he'll buy the company before anyone finds out about her. She's afraid she's ruined everything. She's devastated."

Craig was quiet for a moment, then looked up at Lillian. "I hope she has a nice night." He turned back to his computer and pretended to answer an email.

When he looked up again, Lillian was gone. The office was muted, with only the hum of the air through the vents and the sound of traffic outside.

~

Craig didn't last long alone with his thoughts. He got up from his seat and returned the book to the shelf, then stood at the window. Then he decided to get online and research a new trashcan for his apartment.

That only worked for about four minutes before his mind wandered back to Lillian, back to Rose.

It was impossible for Rose to be in love with him. It was another one of her manipulations. It had to be.

He almost had himself convinced of it, but the one thing he couldn't reconcile was her being on a date with Brett.

It made no sense. Why would anyone subject themselves to that man's presence? Let alone being in a romantic setting with him?

Rose had already run away from Brett once before. She was filled with glee then, giggling and laughing over pizza, mimicking his drawl and his long, sloppy winks.

There was no way she was on a date with him for her own benefit. The only logical explanation was that she was doing it in some misguided sacrifice. A penance.

He shuddered. As angry as he was with her, that was too much.

Craig paced his office and stopped when he spotted something on his desk – a scrap of paper. Lillian had left her phone number. *In case you change your mind*, she'd written.

He sighed. He wasn't changing his mind, but now he couldn't get the image of Rose trapped in Brett's car out of his mind.

He picked up his phone and sent her a message.

Where is this alleged date?

Lillian answered in minutes.

On his yacht. It's docked in Seattle. She sent me the location and said to send the Coast Guard if she didn't return by sunrise.

What!

What if he decides to sail away with her? The guy is a loose cannon.

I know! I told her not to go. I couldn't stop her.

It didn't make any sense. Rose couldn't go through life being beautiful, smart and funny, good at programming and reading people, just to get on board Brett's ship like a sacrificial lamb.

Unless...

No. She didn't love him. She *couldn't* love him.

His phone dinged, and he picked it up, hoping Lillian would say Rose had gotten away and was heading home.

Instead, there was text from Brett.

You need to tell your employee to get riding or she's fired!

Attached was a picture of a mechanical bull on the deck of a ship.

That settled it. Rose might love him or she might've lost her mind. She might've been trying to trick Brett and over-played her hand.

Whatever it was, he couldn't let it happen. He grabbed his wallet and keys and sprinted out the door.

Chapter Twenty-eight

The old Rose would've done it. The old Rose wouldn't have known how to get out of the ridiculous request to ride a mechanical bull on a yacht, and she would've relented. Given in. Buckled up.

Brett kept pushing. "How can I know if you're the right woman for the job if you ain't got no sense of balance?"

He let out a hee-haw sort of laugh and Rose stared at him. She was perfectly comfortable on the overly cushioned couch. There was a table between them, lit with flames from a propane fire. At least he couldn't touch her.

The old Rose would already be struggling to climb onto the mechanical bull, but the new Rose ignored him, instead looking around at the ship.

From afar, it looked beautiful, all elegance and promises of smooth sailing. Once she'd stepped onto the deck, however, Rose realized the bull wasn't even the worst of it. There was a deer antler chandelier hanging perilously above their heads, there were fake (*she hoped they were fake*) cacti everywhere she looked, and the couch she was sitting on had two-foot fringe blowing in the wind.

Money could not buy class, and it couldn't buy her getting on that fake-bull contraption. "My skills as a matchmaker have nothing to do with riding a bull. In fact, there is zero overlap."

Rose picked up the glass of champagne he'd insisted she take and held it in her hand. She wasn't going to drink it – he'd said it was whiskey-flavored champagne – but it made her statement seem final.

"All right, all right." He chuckled. "I must say, I do admire your dedication to the craft of matchmaking."

"Thank you." Rose hesitated. This was her chance, if only she knew how to take it. "The sooner you buy SerenadeMe, the sooner my skills will be at your disposal."

He raised an eyebrow. "And here I thought you came on this date because you liked me."

"This is not a date. This is a discussion."

Of course, he thought it was a date. Lillian thought the same thing. Rose had never said it was a date – not to *him* – though she could see how agreeing to spend her evening on his boat, the lights twinkling on the water behind them, might suggest romantic intentions.

He leaned forward, the flames dancing and reflecting in his eyes. "Maybe I'd like you for myself?"

"I'm not for sale," Rose said simply. "The company is."

"Fine, fine. What if I just poach you for myself, then? You could be the matchmaker at my company. Forget that old place." He waved a hand. "Nobody can afford to buy them anyway."

"I'm not planning to abandon my–" She stopped. "What do you mean nobody can afford to buy them?"

He rubbed his hands together and shrugged. "Ever since you came along, the place is untouchable. You know that. That's how these things go. Prices go up, valuation goes up – it's too much."

"Are you saying you can't afford to buy SerenadeMe?" Had she come all this way to chase a lame duck?

"I *can* afford to buy it." He made a face and poured himself another glass of whisky champagne. "If the price dropped a bit. That's where you coming to work for me would be a big help."

She stood, the white leather fringe of her seat catching on her leg. "Unbelievable. I thought we were going to talk business and you're trying to come up with a scheme."

He stepped in front of her, blocking her exit. "We *are* talking business. Why are you so loyal to that company? I'll double your salary. Don't you want to bring that smug kid down a peg?"

"Craig? You're doing this to hurt Craig?"

He snorted. "I'm doing this to get him out of the way. He's a dimwit."

"Craig is not a dimwit. He's brilliant."

"Brilliant? Brilliant as a chicken trying to fly with no wings."

"Yeah right! He's got amazing wings! And he's ten times the man you are. He built his company from the ground up, and now he's shooting past you and you can't stand it. You're jealous."

"I'm not jealous, I'm–"

"You are, you're jealous. You want to drag him down. You think you can tear SerenadeMe apart? You think people will walk out on him? His employees love him, the board loves him–"

He cut her off. "And let me guess, you love him, too?" He spoke so forcefully that a blob of saliva spat from his mouth. He drew himself up, looking her up and down.

"Maybe I do love him!" she yelled. "Now get out of my way."

He narrowed his eyes and leaned down to get closer to her face. "Or what? You'll throw me overboard?"

"It wouldn't be far enough," she snarled.

Brett put his hands up and stepped aside. "Fine, but don't ever expect an invitation on my boat again."

"You couldn't drag me back to this nightmare," she said, looking over her shoulder. "This place is chintzier than an Atlantic City casino."

She spun and plowed directly into Craig's chest, knocking herself to the ground.

"I'm so sorry!" she said, looking up at him.

He knelt and took her by the hand. "No, I'm sorry. Didn't mean to get in your way."

Rose could hardly believe what she was seeing. "Are you really here?"

"I think so?" He laughed. "Lillian told me where you were. I was coming to...I don't know. Rescue you? It sounds like you don't need to be rescued."

"Here we go," Brett called out, his voice taunting. "Prince Charming himself. Here to serenade me, Craig? Get me to say I'll buy?"

"It sounds like you can't afford it, Brett," Craig said evenly. He touched a gentle hand to Rose's leg. "Are you okay?"

Her knee was throbbing, but there was no blood. The bruise would come later, a reminder of her great failure. "I'm fine. Just mad I spent any time with this bum."

"I can hear you, you know!" Brett yelled, his accent dropping. "I don't know what you were doing, coming on my boat, trying to lead me on."

"I wasn't leading you on. I was trying to get you to close the sale, you numpty!" She shook her head and lowered her voice. "The nerve of some people."

Craig took her by the hands and helped her up. "I never should've let him in the building. I'm sorry."

"It's okay." She shook her head. "It's my fault. I got desperate."

He laughed. "I can see that."

"Let's get out of here." Rose dusted herself off and started walking – off the ship, down the stairs, down the dock and as far away as she could get. She wanted to run from her embarrassment and her shame, and run away from crying, too.

Craig followed.

They were back on the street, the quiet storefronts lighting the night. Rose felt like she wasn't going to cry, for once. She stopped and turned to look at him. "Listen, Craig, I'm sorry about that. I'll do everything I can to find a buyer, and then you'll never have to see me again."

He stared at her, his eyes searching hers. "How much of that did you mean?"

She tilted her head. "When I was yelling at Brett?"

He nodded.

Oh. This was awkward. "How much of it did you hear?"

A smile crossed his face and he squinted. "Everything?"

Rose looked down at her shoes before forcing herself to look into his eyes again. "Everything, then. I think you're brilliant, and I love – *loved* – working at SerenadeMe. I never meant to ruin it."

He opened his mouth to speak, but she held up a hand. "Let me finish. This is the last time I'll bother you." She took a deep breath and steadied her thoughts. "I swear I never meant to lie, and I never meant for it to go this far. I should've told you sooner, but I didn't.

"There's no excuse. I messed up. I'm not a confident person, Craig. I was trying to be someone new, someone different. Someone who could be happy.

"I stayed in my last job for *way* too long. I was used to being miserable, and I'd never been this happy before. I loved coming to work and seeing you. I loved matching clients. I even loved the weekly meetings with the programmers!"

Her voice fell quiet as he stared into her eyes.

She hadn't put it into words before, but this was it. This was the truth, just as she knew it. "I pretended to be someone I wasn't, and I think it's because I liked who that person was. I could really *be* somebody, not just sad old Rose."

His gentle gaze settled on her, his eyes shining in the night. "You *are* somebody, Rose. All the success you had was yours. That was you. That was really *you*."

"Yeah." She scoffed. "I really messed things up."

"No, you didn't. I overreacted because I'm insecure. I was afraid I'd ruin the company, and I lashed out at you, but it was stupid. I like you, Rose. Whoever you are."

The tears were threatening to make an appearance, flooding her eyes and blurring her vision. "Thanks. I like you, too."

He took a step closer. "'Like' me? I think, and correct me if I'm wrong, you told Brett you love me."

A laugh burst out of her. "Ah, did I? That doesn't sound like me."

He nodded. "I think it does."

She looked down. "If I hadn't cared about you, I never would've told you the truth."

"I know."

"I never meant for it to go this far."

He nodded. "I know."

"If I could take back what I did..."

Craig delicately brushed his hand against her cheek. "Please don't."

He leaned in, his lips against hers with the softest touch, like a butterfly taking off.

"I love you, too," he whispered, pulling away ever so slightly.

She smiled, biting her lip. "Really? Did you mean Rose Woodson or Rose Woodley? Because we've had some confusion."

"I mean you. I like you for you. I'd be with you any day, any time, I don't need anything from you. I just love you."

Her breath caught in her throat. "Well, then." She got up on her tiptoes and kissed him back.

Epilogue

Weddings at The Grand Madrona Hotel would never get old to Claire. The hotel was stunning on a normal day, but when the flowers and presents and guests poured in, it was like something out of a dream.

Today was even more special because it was Marty and Emma's wedding. Chip had volunteered to help with preparations, and for the week leading up to the wedding, Lucy chased him around, pointing and sending him up ladders.

Under her watchful eye, he decorated the ballroom, stringing thousands of twinkling lights, draping flowing cloths, and hanging fresh greenery from high above.

"Okay, that's crooked," Lucy would bark. "You need to fix it!"

Chip never argued, but he did tease. "It doesn't look crooked to me. Maybe your vision is off. I think you need glasses."

"You need glasses if you can't see how twisted that is!" Lucy would yell.

Claire just stood back and laughed. Lucy had a real talent for event planning. After the wedding, she was going to ask her to sign on officially to help people plan their events at the hotel.

Their bookings were up four hundred percent, and Claire needed backup. Lucy could use a change, too – she was getting bored at the farm again, and nothing good came of Lucy being bored.

With the preparations over, it was time to just enjoy. Marty and Emma had opted to keep things small, which was fine with Claire. Her sister Becca had made it, of course, for the wedding, along with Marty's adoptive parents and Emma's family. There was a smattering of old friends, and the ceremony had been beautiful and peaceful atop Mt. Constitution, the world unfolding beneath them.

Back at the hotel, the band was playing, the sun was setting, and couples were taking to the dance floor. Lillian and Dustin were already dancing. Rob managed to pull Lucy onto the dance floor, away from nitpicking details, and Rose and Craig were whispering in the corner.

Claire was so happy for her. She'd found herself in the last year and finally seemed comfortable in her own skin. She'd arrived in a stunning floor-length lilac gown with delicate flowers embroidered at the seam – Lucy's choice, apparently.

Rose blew a kiss before being pulled onto the dance floor herself. Thanks to her, Craig had been able to sell the company to a guy named Phoenix while staying on as an executive. Rose kept her matchmaking going, even training new staff in her art. She had come clean about the case of mistaken identity, and as Claire had hoped, no one cared. All they cared about was what she did for the company, and there she was infallible.

Claire stood back and looked at the ballroom. There was a feeling in her chest she couldn't name, a warmth coming from her heart. Everyone she loved was in this room. Everyone was, in this moment, happy. She was finally home.

There was a tap on her shoulder, and she turned to see Chip, tall and handsome in his navy blue suit. "Is the beautiful lady available for a dance?"

She put her hand in his. "For you? Always."

The Next Chapter

Not ready to leave the magic of the San Juan Islands? Neither is author Amelia Addler! Join her in the next series, The Spotted Cottage Series, set on San Juan Island with *The Spotted Cottage by the Sea*.

Introduction to
The Spotted Cottage by the Sea

A broke divorcée, a handsome movie star, and a secret threatening to ruin it all...

When 50-year old Sheila hears about her ex-husband's scheme to sell his mother's seaside cottage and tea shop, she jumps into action. Moving in with her beloved mother-in-law Patty is the easy part – the real challenge arises when she discovers the potential buyer is none other than the handsome movie star Russell Westwood who's just moved in next door.

Russell doesn't want trouble. He moved to San Juan Island to find peace after his Hollywood-famous wife left him, and that peace doesn't include an angry Sheila at his door. Little by little, though, Russell finds himself pulled in by Sheila's unassuming charm and questioning his resolve to stay single.